Wondering While Wandering

Sandra Waggoner

Wagon Tracks
PUBLISHING

Especially for my Hubby

I know when God planned Greg for me and me for Greg, He had a twinkle in his eye and laughter in his heart.

Galatians 5:22 and 23 put in black and white what we live in color. "But the fruit of the Spirit is love, joy, peace, longsuffering, gentleness, goodness, faith, meekness, temperance: against such there is no law."

Love is Greg telling me I am beautiful in the morning when I crawl out of bed. Joy is when I look in the mirror, and that beauty is splayed, pillow-tossed hair and baggage beneath my eyes. Peace is knowing he really means I am beautiful because he knows my heart. Longsuffering is 46 years of still married. Gentleness is when he catches my eye across the room, and it spreads that special smile reserved for only me. Goodness is handing me an Almond Joy candy bar when I am on a diet, and faith is loving me just the way I am. Temperance is biting his tongue when I am grouchy and with his thumb gently wiping a tear from my eye.

Greg is God's special gift to me, and I thank my Lord for him every single day. Only God can make such gifts!

God's Word
Wondering While Wandering

God's Word is infallible.

My stories are not.

God spoke His words in black and white.

My words are like running through spring pastures dotted with brilliantly colored flowers.

God's words are truth.

My words are feelings.

In no way do I put my words above God's.

He is my Lord, my Saviour, and my King.

I am His servant, and I am honored to be used in His service.

Sandra Waggoner

Wondering While Wandering

Wondering While Wandering

Table of Contents

A Baby, a Stable, God's Time 9

After the Cross 25

Beautiful Feet 37

I Go a Fishing 49

Jochebed 65

Living Water 75

Naaman 85

Sweet Baby's Breath 103

The Carpenter 117

The Perfect Lamb 131

The Roman Soldier 137

King Solomon's Wisdom 147

Wondering While Wandering

Wondering While Wandering

A Baby, a Stable, God's Time

Luke 2:1-7

She was standing at the window when the sharp pain struck. She took a deep breath and counted on her fingers. Eight. Time told her she was right. Her body was screaming otherwise. Should she tell her espoused husband? She watched him step from the shop and shake hands with her father. As soon as her father was out of sight Joseph studied the hammer he held then slung it across the hard ground. It hit the side of the chicken yard, and the scared fowl scattered and squawked up a dusty storm.

No, she would not tell Joseph. Something was bothering him. She plunged her hands into the bread dough easing her emotions by kneading the bread. Who was she fooling? Something had been bothering him ever since she had told him about the baby. He hardly talked to her, and she longed to see again the look in his eyes which told her she was everything to him.

Wondering While Wandering

It was gone, and she prayed God would bring it back.

Joseph knocked on the door before he thrust it open and stepped into the small room. He asked her mother if he might speak with her daughter and was surprised when her mother meekly left the room.

Joseph crossed to the table, yanked out a chair, and sat.

Mary smiled. He never did anything quietly. That must be the man in him.

"Come sit down, Mary. We need to talk." He drummed his fingers on the table, but he did not lift his eyes to look at her.

Mary rubbed the dough from her hands and was glad to sit. She reached over and scooped up his fingers to quiet them. "Joseph?" she questioned.

He glanced quickly at her and let his troubled eyes stray. "Mary, we have a problem."

Mary had never seen Joseph cry, but she thought he was not far from it.

He drew his hand from hers and rubbed his forehead. "It is about that tax

Wondering While Wandering

law. Caesar Augustus passed the thing. It requires us to go to our own city to be taxed. I tried, Mary, but there was no way to let you stay here. We are espoused, promised. I have to take you with me to Bethlehem." He shook his head, and Mary thought the tears would fly. For a moment he struggled, swallowed, and continued, "Mary, I am sorry. I have prayed, but still, we must go." He paused and for once he looked into her eyes with a touch of the love she remembered, "Can you make it, Mary? I know you have at least a month before this baby comes, but it will be hard for you to travel. Do you think you can make it?"

Mary nodded, "I must. Maybe we could borrow your father's ox cart? It would make it easier?"

Joseph stood, turned his back, and spread his hands. He sighed, "Mary, my father does not believe me about this baby being God's son. He threw me out of the house. He refuses to see me or talk to me. He will not even let my mother, or my sisters and brothers speak to me."

"Joseph! I am sorry," Mary whispered. She knew the feeling of being shunned. No

11

one talked to her anymore, at the well, at the market, anywhere.

Joseph's shoulders slumped. "Sometimes, Mary... sometimes, I wish the Lord had not chosen you and me. Do you ever feel that way?"

The tears Joseph held back Mary let flow. "Joseph, sometimes. Sometimes, I do wish Jehovah had not chosen us, but then I remember who this baby is." She crossed to her intended. "Joseph, put your hand here and feel." She took his hand and placed it on her rounded tummy. She smiled as the baby kicked bouncing Joseph's hand away. "This baby is the prophesy Isaiah gave, the promised Messiah, the King of Kings. Joseph this is the Son of God. It is an honor that God chose you and me."

Joseph pulled his hand away with words he refused to say. It was not his baby, and he was fighting the feelings he had. How did a man love a woman and watch her have another's baby...even if it was God's son? Quickly he looked to the roof hiding his heart from Mary. "You will have to ride Ben. He is an old, cranky donkey. He is slow, but he is all I have got. It will be rough, and I am sorry. If we leave tomorrow, early, it will give us extra time. Can you do that?"

Mary shrugged, "Joseph, I must."

Joseph nodded. "Then we leave early, very early in the morning. I pray all goes well," he turned to the door.

"Joseph, this baby is God's son. It will go well because God will protect us," Mary gently spoke to the back of her promised husband. He did not say a word as he shoved the door open and left.

Mary's mother looked at the floor in despair when her daughter told her she must go with Joseph to Bethlehem. How could one argue with Caesar?

Finally, the restless night passed, and morning came too early. Everything seemed to take extra time. The road was busy with hordes of people going to be taxed just as they were. Yet it was a breath of fresh air when strangers were friendly. Most travelers passed them on the way, and Joseph was kind and concerned stopping to rest many times. As evening shadows fell, they were the only travelers left on the road.

Wondering While Wandering

Mary kept the pains to herself so as not to worry Joseph. Joseph dropped the leading reins to the side of Ben and stepped back to check on his espoused wife. "You look worn out, Mary. Just hold on a little longer, and I promise a soft bed in Bethlehem."

As she nodded, Mary held her breath. She was more than worn out. Her body was cringing with pain, and like it or not, this baby was going to come, and it might be any time now.

Joseph started Ben again, and Mary felt each swaying step he took with a jolt. Before long she was afraid she wouldn't care if she had this baby in the roadside ditch. A velvety black cloaked the sky, while slowly the stars blinked to open and shine.

Mary did not wonder that they were the only ones left on the road. It would be better to have the baby without a crowd about.

When Joseph moved beside her, she did not know, but somehow he was holding her onto Ben and guiding the donkey from his side. "It's time for the baby, isn't it,

Wondering While Wandering

Mary? I counted only eight months, but it is time, isn't it?"

Sweat trickled down her dusty face. She could not hide the pain anymore. She nodded brushing her hand over her cheeks smearing the dust and sweat into thin steaks of mud.

"How long do we have?" he asked.

"I do not know, Joseph. I've never done this before." She held her bottom lip between her teeth as another tremor ripped through her body.

"Try to hold on, Mary. We are on the outskirts of Bethlehem. We will find a room, and I will go for help," Joseph soothed her.

Mary could not answer. She was gulping in great breaths of air as the pain stretched on.

Joseph handed her the reins. "Hold on, Mary, I see an inn, right there." He twisted the lead rope about her hand, ran, and pounded at the door.

From beyond her world, Mary listened to pieces of the exchange.

Wondering While Wandering

"I have got to have a room!"

"Sir, there is not a room to be had in all of Bethlehem. This city is full up and overflowing."

"But...you do not understand. My Mary is going to have a baby... right now!" His panicked voice rose.

The tired woman sighed, "Sir, I would like to help..."

Joseph clutched her arm. "Please, please. I don't know what to do, but I have got to get her off that donkey, and I must get her help."

From behind the woman a clear, young voice spoke, "Mether, I could clean out a stall in the stable. I could throw fresh straw down for her?"

"Son, you are supposed to be with the flock. You better get back before your father finds you here," his Mether scolded him.

"Mether, Levi is with the flock. I am to come back in a bit, but Mether look. The lady needs a place. She is going to have a baby," he pleaded.

Wondering While Wandering

His mether looked to Joseph, pushed her hair away from her face, and sighed. "Will a stall in the stable do?"

Joseph did not know a stray tear had escaped. Wildly he shook her hand, "Yes! Oh yes! Thank you! Thank you! What is the cost?"

"Later, sir. We will take care of payment later. It looks like you had better get your wife to the stable quick." She turned to her son, "Darius, show them to the stable, and get things ready. I will get your sister to fetch hot water and rags."

"Yes, thank you, thank you. We do not have anything. The baby is not due for another month," Joseph whispered.

With a weary smile she reached out and patted his hand, "Sir, sometimes our timing is off, but God's timing never is. His is always perfect."

Joseph swallowed, turned, and ran to catch Mary as she swayed from the donkey's back. "We have got a place, Mary. It is only a stable stall, will that work?"

Wondering While Wandering

Sweetly she smiled, "It is going to have to work, Joseph, My water just broke."

Joseph's eyes grew. He stumbled into a run as he followed the shepherd boy to the stable. "There is no time for clean-up, Darius." Quickly he kicked the soiled straw away and let Darius pitch new straw in its place. Gently he laid Mary down.

Mary squeezed his hand. He did not know she had such strength. When she eased her grip he told her, "I have got to go get help, Mary. I do not know how to deliver a baby."

With both hands Mary grabbed him and pulled him to her, "No you do not. You cannot leave me. I have carried this baby alone, and I will not have him without you. God gave you to me. I need you to help me. I need you, Joseph."

Joseph was scared, but he dared not move from her side. He stroked her gently. "Darius?" he called over his shoulder, "I need light. I have got to see what I am doing."

Wondering While Wandering

Darius ran to the door and pulled it wide. In awe he gasped as light flooded into the stable from the night sky.

"Thanks, Darius, just bring that lamp over here."

Darius held his hands wide, "I don't have no lamp. That is some special star lighting up the whole sky."

"Wow!" Darius's sister trudged into the stable with a bucket of steaming water and a pile of rags slung over her shoulder. She stopped beside Joseph, "Wow! That is some star shining out there!" She plopped the bucket down. "Mether says she is sorry. The only clean thing she has left in the house is this pile of swaddling clothes we keep for the sacrifice lambs. She says she won't be offended if you don't want to use these grave clothes for your baby. But they are clean, and that is all she's got."

Joseph whispered in desperation, "Thank you, Little One. Do you think your Mether would come help?"

"Little One?" The little girl blinked. "I am not so little. I can do stuff as good as my brothers," she giggled. "And my name is

19

Wondering While Wandering

Jerico." She placed her lips in a firm line. "And," she considered, "Mether help? Maybe," Jerico shrugged, "but she has a big pile of dirty dishes, but I'd be glad to stay and help." The girl smiled showing a new tooth crowding into an empty spot.

Darius laughed as his sister climbed the stall fence to 'help'. "Jerico, you are nosy, and you just want to watch and get out of helping Mether with the dishes."

"Joseph!" Mary called and groaned. "This baby is coming."

All time swarmed and stood still at once. Joseph had never been so busy in his life. He caught the baby. He cut the cord. He washed the infant and gently wrapped the baby in the clean, swaddling clothes.

"You do not mind the swaddling clothes?" he asked as he placed the baby in Mary's arms. We were not prepared. You were only eight months along."

"Joseph," she reached up to stroke his face, "Isn't eight the number of new beginnings? This is certainly a new beginning for you and me, and maybe the whole world."

Wondering While Wandering

She fingered the swaddling clothes. Sorrow seized her eyes, and tears frosted them. "Grave clothes? For the Son of God? Joseph?" She paused as little shivers of apprehension ran through her body. "Grave clothes...I guess I mind a little. It scares me. I wonder what death clothes means?" She stroked the soft hair of her new little babe and touched her lips to his cheek. She opened his hand. "Joseph, I wonder what mysteries he holds in these tiny hands? I think he may hold our future in these hands. She looked over to her promised husband, "Do you want to hold him?"

Cold distance clouded Joseph's face, "Mary," he whispered in a torn voice. "He is not my son."

She flashed her eyes and took a deep breath. She studied Joseph's torn face as she composed her words. "Joseph, he is not really my son either. He is God's son. God just used me as the gift wrap to deliver His gift to this world."

Tears were flooding Joseph's hardened face. He licked his lips, nodded and stretched his arms out to hold the son God had chosen to share with him. This baby was God's son... but God had placed this baby in his care for a short time.

Mary softly spoke, "He needs us, Joseph. He needs both of us. He needs us to protect this perfect little gift."

Joseph nodded.

A smile spread over the new mother's face, "I am glad God chose you, Joseph. With your heart and your life, you will care for our little Messiah, God's precious gift to all mankind."

A twinkle flared in Joseph's eye, "And God chose the most beautiful gift wrap on the face of this earth to wrap his son in. I love you, Mary."

Mary swallowed. That was the look she had missed from Joseph's eyes for so long. It was the look that proclaimed he loved her, and the look she had prayed God would let her see again. "Thank you, Lord God," she looked to the rafters and smiled.

From the fence, Jerico gaped in awe. The skies burst with music. Darius led a group of shepherds quietly through the open door, and the little baby stretched out his arms and smiled.

Wondering While Wandering

After the Cross
Matthew 27:51-53

If Timna had thought the worst was over she now knew she had been wrong. She dropped her head in her hands and rubbed her forehead to ease away the sights and sounds which were agony. It had been a long few days, and she did not think anything could wipe her memory clean.

There was a scratching on the other side of the door and a low, gruff voice, "Timna, quick, open the door."

Chills spread over Timna's body. She would know that voice anywhere.

"Come on, woman, we know you are in there. We will bust the door down if we have to."

'We?' That meant he was not alone. She slipped over to the water pot and grabbed the knife she kept beside it before she went to the door. Timna leaned against the rough wood and hissed, "What do you want?"

"We want in. We need in. This city ain't exactly friendly toward us now." He

25

did not wait for her to open the door. He gave a mighty shove throwing the door wide and knocking Timna off balance. She stumbled, tossed her hands wildly whipping the knife through the air.

In horror the man gasped, "What was that for? You barely missed my throat!"

Timna clutched the knife, "This city has not been friendly to me either. No one talks to me. They stare at me from a distance. They drop their heads when I pass, and Merchants will not sell to me. So, if you have come for food, I have none to give."

"We have bread. We need shelter, woman, a place to hide. You owe us that much."

"I do not owe you anything. You owe me. My husband kept silent for your sake. He kept his secret to the death, and it was not a pleasant death either. Were you there, Mathias? Did you watch him hang on that horrible cross? Did you watch him struggle for one more breath?"

Mathias spread his hands and shook his head, "It was awful, and, yes, I saw the most of it. But Timna, you must believe me. There was nothing I could do."

Wondering While Wandering

Timna dropped the hand that held the knife and wiped tears from her face with the other.

Without taking his eyes from hers he lowered his voice and gruffly called, "Come on in, comrades."

Silently three more of the old crew slipped into the room to huddle in an empty corner. The last man, a fourth, closed the door and threw the bolt in place before he joined the others. A dark cloak covered him from hood to dirt floor.

Timna watched in silence.

Mathias broke the silence, "I know you was Lucas's woman."

"I was not just his woman. I was his wife," she corrected.

"Yes, begging your pardon, his wife. Look, Timna, he told us you were pretty good at fixing wounds, and this one," he nodded toward the cloaked figure, "this one needs your help in a bad way."

The man dropped the hood from his head and Timna gasped. "For all that is holy! What happened to you?"

A wicked gash bolted from the top of his head, jumped over an empty eye socket and on down his face. Black and blue and blood colored his swollen jaw, and it looked to be oozing some. The man tried to answer from one side of his mouth. "I was in the temple when the curtain was torn in twain. The bar caught the side of my head and ripped up my face."

Timna clutched her throat. "That was crucifixion day. The news of the vale in the temple being torn in half traveled over the whole city, and you were in there?"

He nodded.

She paused remembering the earthquake and the darkening of the sky. She narrowed her eyes, "Are you a priest then? I am sure you could get better help than me."

The men in the corner broke into a volley of laughter as they sunk to the floor making themselves at home.

"A priest?"

"That's a good one!"

"By all that's mighty, him, a priest!"

Timna narrowed her eyes, "You are not a priest? Then who are you? And what were you doing in the temple? Oh." She thrust her hand over her heart, "I'm sorry. Were you praying for a loved one? Did you have someone you loved hung on one of those crosses that day? A brother? A cousin?" Timna stretched out a gentle hand to comfort him.

Mathias cackled, "Yeah, he had someone he loved. He loved that one they called the King of the Jews, didn't you, man?"

The one-eyed man glared at Mathias.

Mathias waved toward the unhooded man, "I don't really have any sympathy for you. None of the rest of us thought it was a good plan. We tried in vain to talk you out of it."

The man rolled back his lips as a hungry wolf and spoke through slits in his teeth because his mouth would not open all the way, "I'll not split the goods with you then."

"If you don't get that face fixed you won't be 'splitting the goods' with any the one of us," Mathias reminded him.

The man clouted his fists towards Mathias, and Mathias with wrath moved to meet him.

Timna stepped between them. "Not in my home, and you had best tell me what happened, so I know what kind of trouble to expect from the authorities."

Wondering While Wandering

Silence flooded the room.

"No one wants to talk? Very well," Timna walked to the door, unlatched it, and opened it to the black night. "All of you, out. Maybe Hell itself has a better hiding place for the lot of you."

One of the men sitting on the floor blared out, "It was his idea." He sliced his finger through the air to point at the wounded man.

The man growled and took a violent step toward him.

The man shuttered, searched for a back door, and found none. "Well, I didn't want to go along with the idea, but I was out voted."

"And what was this idea?" Timna still held the door wide.

Mathias answered, "Close the door, and we will tell you all."

Slowly Timna shut the door, she but kept her hand on the latch.

Mathias pulled in a deep breath and began, "Him, Rueben, it was what had the idea." He pointed to the grizzled man huddled on the floor. "You see, he figured while everyone was watching the hangings, we was to rob the temple. He knew where all the money bags and boxes were kept, beings he studied the law for a while before he got kicked out. Unholy he was, and tossed in prison for robbing the widows when they would come to pray. But he guessed no one would be in the temple. "Everybody will be watching the crucifixion," he said. And he was right. We was all alone in the temple when some kind of holy storm busted through there ripping that curtain apart. The earth was shaking, but not as much as I was. There was no one in the temple but the five of us, yet I think it was mighty crowded...maybe...maybe an army of angels we couldn't see." The man's eyes bulged with fear.

"I think it was God himself!" the man huddled on the floor who once studied to be a priest burst out as he blasted to his dancing feet. He whipped about spewing a wildly insane look.

The other two men on the floor scooted further from him.

"You robbed the temple?" Timna was appalled.

The three on the floor dropped their heads. Mathias shrugged and nodded to the cloaked man, "He's the leader, and he thought it was a good idea."

Wondering While Wandering

Timna turned to the man, "Just who are you? No one robs the temple. Do you not fear God Almighty? And do you know what those religious leaders will do to you if they catch you? You must have seen at least part of what they did to that man they called Jesus, and they could not even prove anything against him. And, you," she pointed the knife at the wounded man, "Mathias said you cared for the one they called the King of the Jews. You could not have cared." She thrust her hand in the air. "Get out. Get out of my house! I will not be near you when they find you because I do not want any part of the trouble you will bring to me."

"Timna, for Lucas, your husband's memory, couldn't you do this one thing for us?" Mathias pleaded.

"For my husband's sake? You, I know, Mathias, and the three of you? I would recognize your hangdog faces anywhere, but I know you ran with my husband. I told Lucas to stay away from the lot of you because you were no good, and I was right. Look what happened to my Lucas!" She turned to the man with the torn face. "But you I do not know. What were you to my Lucas?"

Wondering While Wandering

His one eye was direct, "I met him in prison. We were chained to the same rock wall."

Timna looked him up and down. "Prison? You robbed the temple? You cared for Jesus? How could you have cared for Jesus? He was never in prison. Most say he was an innocent man. You could not have even known Jesus."

A thick pause settle about the room until Mathias broke it with a whisper, "Go on, man. Tell her."

With the one hollow eye focused on the woman, he swallowed and said, "That Jesus, he gave his life for mine." The man pounded his chest accenting each word. "I was the people's choice. I was the one set free. My name is Barabbas, but... if Jesus truly had been the Son of God no one could have killed him. No one could have killed him. He would not be dead."

Timna stood tall pointing the knife. "Could they have not killed him? Have you not studied the scriptures? Have you not heard it prophesied that one would die for all?"

The man who had studied the law to become a priest jumped from the dirt floor. "Maybe that is why the curtain of the temple was torn asunder! Maybe this Jesus was the Son of God!"

Barabbas hissed, "If he had been the Son of God I tell you I would have not been set free and he would not have died on that cross!"

Timna's heart began throbbing in her throat. The last few days were swirling in her head. How she had wished over and over again that it had been Lucas set free, but no. It had been this...this man, Barabbas, the thief and murderer. Barabbas had been the lucky one, not her Lucas. She was shaking as she yanked the door as wide as it would go with one hand and swung the knife she still held in the other. Tears bathed her face as her heart was rung out of life itself. "Get out. All of you!" She whispered it slowly. "Get out."

But...

No one moved. She watched the three men on the floor pale. Mathias took a shaking step backward, but Barabbas gasped and dropped to the dirt floor on his knees. All the hardened criminals were staring out into the night through the open door.

Timna slowly followed their gaze. She dropped the knife and threw her hand over her mouth. "Lucas? Lucas? It cannot be. I watched you die on that cross."

Gently he spoke, "Timna, love, listen to me. I did die on that cross, but I am alive. I want you to meet someone I met while hanging on that cross." He turned to motion to a man still standing in the dark. "Timna, this is Jesus, the King of the Jews, and believe me, He can explain it better than I can. He took me with him to Paradise, Timna, just as he promised he would do!"

Matthew 27:51-53 "And, behold, the veil of the temple was rent in twain from the top to the bottom; and the earth did quake, and the rocks rent; And the graves were opened; and many bodies of the saints which slept arose, And came out of the graves after his resurrection, and went into the holy city, and appeared unto many."

Wondering While Wandering

Wondering While Wandering

Beautiful Feet

Luke 16:19-31

The beggar stood watching the gate from across the street. He remembered those iron bars with cold and foreboding.

The man beside the beggar gave a slight shake of the head. "Not yet, Son," he whispered as he motioned up the street.

A man clad in rich garments strolled their way.

The Beggar took in a deep breath. That was one of the brothers, Simeon. The Beggar would know him anywhere. Simeon, the hardhearted brother who kicked the dogs and threw bread or bones just to watch the scramble and fight between the animals. It was just like old times. When Simeon was close enough to the gate, he yanked a wad from his pocket and unfolded the cloth to display a hunk of bread slavered with butter and spices. He whistled to the dogs and threw the bread over their heads to hit the rock wall and slide to the ground leaving a trail of butter on the stone wall as would a slug. The dogs leaped, snarled, and fought for the trophy. Simeon watched with amusement. An old

Wondering While Wandering

gray dog yelped as he was pushed from the fight. He tucked his tail and limped to the wall to lick his wounds but found the streak of butter. He raised to his hind legs and lapped at the wall. It did not fill his belly. It only tantalized him to whine and wish for more, but that would be his share for today. Simeon laughed, called at the gate and stepped inside.

The man in the shadows beside The Beggar spoke, "Son, I believe he is the last to come. Are you ready to do this?"

The Beggar nodded. "I have to try. There are not many who get a chance like this."

The man gave his approval. "I will wait here for you, Son. Remember, I have your back."

"Thank you."

The Beggar took a gulp of air and walked toward the gate but stopped when the dogs surrounded him. Some snarled low while others whined. The old gray dog slunk to his side and licked at The Beggar's foot. The man bent down to scuff the dog behind his ears, "You remember me, don't you, Ole Boy?"

Wondering While Wandering

The gray dog whined and flopped his mangy tail. The Beggar reached into his cloak and pulled out a treat he had saved for this dog. "Here you go, Ole Boy. I did not forget you, either."

In one gulp, the broken dog swallowed it down, merging it with a moan of thanks from deep within.

The Beggar took a deep breath, stepped to the gate, and called.

It was the cold hearted brother, Simeon, who came. His chilly eyes traveled up and down The Beggar before he spoke, "We allow no beggars here. Be on your way. We have nothing for you."

The Beggar held up his hand, "Wait. It is I who have something for you."

Simeon narrowed his eyes in disbelief, "You, a beggar? You have something I would want?"

"Yes. I have a message from your brother."

A light glinted in Simeon's eyes as they traveled from the top of his head to his bare feet. He leaned back and crossed his arms.

Wondering While Wandering

"Really? What message could you, a beggar, have from a brother of mine? Especially since all of us are here, met to settle our deceased brother's estate." He stopped to chuckled under his breath, "This message must be from one of us, then." He waved over his shoulder and called, "Brothers, I need all of you here, now!"

As the other brothers gathered, The Beggar tensed. The old dog laid his head on The Beggar's foot and whined to comfort his companion.

"It will be fine, Ole Boy, I promise you, it will be fine," The Beggar spoke low and prayed it would be fine. "If only they will listen to me." He pushed his lips in a grim line.

Simeon swung his hand to include all his brothers, "This is our oldest brother, Matthew, Job, Noah, and Shechem. So, which of these, my brothers, sent you with a message for me?"

The four men who had come to their brother's aid had the same looks of the man The Beggar carried the message from. All bear the cold, hardened look in their eyes as they scrutinized him.

The Beggar stood to his full height. His heart pounded faster now, but nothing could harm him. This message was so important he had to be bold. It could affect all these men.

"Well, out with it, man. Which of my brothers here, sent you with this much important message?"

The Beggar widened his eyes and let the words flow. "None of these. It was your brother who lived in this very place."

"What? In this place? How dare you?" Simeon seethed.

"Now we know you lie!" the red-bearded brother growled.

Fists were balled, and anger shot from eyes.

"Our brother has been dead for over two weeks!"

"And you say you have a message from him?" the oldest snapped.

"Just how could he have sent you with a message for us?"

The Beggar took a step toward them, "And so have I been dead...along with your brother."

"What?" Shechem wailed.

Wondering While Wandering

"You make no sense, man!" Noah belted.

"Lunatic!" Job spat.

"How could you and he be dead, and you come with a message from him for us?"

"Call the soldiers!" A brother started to swing the gate shut.

"Wait," The Beggar held up his hand, "Your brother wanted you to know," he paused to look directly at the brethren. "He wanted you to know Hell is real, but you do not have to go there."

Simeon lashed toward him. His brothers held him back, "Simeon, find out what he means, first." Matthew tightened his grip on his brother's arm.

"I know what he means." Anger turned his voice into a growl. "He is saying he saw our brother in Hell...in Hell, because that is the only place a dead beggar like him could go."

"In Hell?" Shechem gasped.

"Hell? Hell? Hell!" Echoes of the word spread through the thick rage.

"Yes," The Beggar whispered. "In Hell."

Wondering While Wandering

"You lie!" Simeon spat on the ground.

"Our brother would not go to Hell... Paradise, yes, but never Hell."

"He never missed a Sabbath," Noah boasted.

"He was the most religious man I know!"

"He gave his tithes and offerings," Job added.

"Why he even let beggars gather at his gate! God dare not send him to Hell," Simeon roared.

The Beggar interrupted the list of good their brother had done. "God did not send your brother to Hell. It was your brother's choice. But your brother wanted you to know that you have that same choice. You must put your faith and your trust and your sins in the hands of Jesus Christ..."

"Jesus Christ? Put our trust in Jesus Christ? You are mad, or you must have been dead because everyone around here knows Jesus Christ was crucified days ago," Simeon snarled.

The old gray dog growled as he inched closer to protect his friend.

Wondering While Wandering

Quietly, The Beggar spoke, "Oh, I know Jesus Christ was crucified, but I also know he lives. It was Jesus Christ who emptied Paradise and brought me here, to your brother's house today."

The old dog thumped his tail as though applauding, hailing dust to rise in the silent adoration.

"Wait," Simeon clutched his throat. "Could it be?" He stepped face to face with the beggar, searching his eyes. He swallowed and mumbled, "No...no...no." Simeon backed away, "I do recognize you! You are that man, the beggar who wallowed here at my brother's gate."

Immediately, The Beggar was surrounded by all the brothers and examined.

"I tell you, he is the one," Simeon heaved from deep within.

Job whispered, "Simeon is right! This is the body Matthew and I dragged away the day our brother died. It has to be him."

"You are that beggar?" Matthew whispered with a tremor in his voice. "But you were dead. We drug you away."

Wondering While Wandering

Simeon asked, "Wait! What is your name? I know it, but you must say it for me to believe."

"My given name is Lazarus."

Simeon choked on his words, "Lazarus? Lazarus! It is you?"

The brothers were appalled, and the circle grew tighter.

"Get out!"

"Take him to the authorities!"

"Stone him!" They yelled.

Lazarus shook his head, "You cannot take me, but I plead with you to listen. I did beg at your brother's gate, but in Hell your brother begged at mine."

"Our brother, a beggar in Hell?"

"For what would he beg? He had everything."

"Yes, he had everything...in this life, yet he has nothing but torments in Hell. He does not want you to come there. Your brother begged me to carry a drop of water on the tip of my finger to quench his thirst."

"He begged for water? Water? That makes no sense," Simeon shook his head.

Wondering While Wandering

Lazarus was nose-to-nose with Simeon, "There is no water in Hell. Jesus Christ is the living water, and Jesus is not in Hell. Your brother felt that if I, being from the dead, came with a message from him, you would believe on Jesus Christ as the only begotten Son of God, The Living Water, and the only way to Heaven."

Simeon gasped in awe.

One of the brothers grabbed Simeon's arm and shook him. "Simeon, you cannot believe this beggar! He lies!"

Simeon blinked and rubbed his hand over his brow, "I don't know, almost, maybe..."

The old gray dog at Lazarus's feet whined.

From behind there was a soft call, "Lazarus, time to be on our way."

Lazarus drew in a deep breath, "Yes, Master." As he turned to go he whispered, "Though one rose from the dead...I had so hoped..."

Silence fell. A gasp ripped through the quiet. "Did you see who he walked with? Did you see? It looked to be Jesus Christ, the one who was crucified!"

Wondering While Wandering

A smile rippled across Lazarus' face. "Maybe? Lord, maybe? Maybe some will believe you rose from the dead!"

The man beside him put a scarred hand on his shoulder, "That is the plan, Son. That is the plan. Lazarus, For whosoever shall call upon the name of the Lord shall be saved. How then shall they call on him in whom they have not believed? and how shall they believe in him of whom they have not heard? and how shall they hear without a preacher? And how shall they preach, except they be sent? as it is written, How beautiful are the feet of them that preach the gospel of peace, and bring glad tidings of good things!"

Down the street, the old gray dog followed the beautiful feet of The Beggar in step with his Saviour.

In a frenzy, dogs yelped and scattered as the iron gates were thrust open and crashed against the stone wall. "Wait," Simeon yelled with his hands waving and his garments flying, "Wait, I believe!"

Wondering While Wandering

Wondering While Wandering

I Go a Fishing

John 21:1-19

He kicked the covers off and sat on the edge of the bed, his elbows propped on his knees and his pounding head thrust in his rugged hands. Nothing would ever be the same.

His wife stirred, rolled over and yawned. "Love," she laid a gentle hand on his shoulder, "it is early, Love. Come back to bed."

"Early? For a fisherman? Late is what it is." His blurry eyes looked at nothing and saw clearly things he wished he could forget. He jerked his hands through his hair and stood.

His wife stretched. "I'll fix something for you to eat."

In the dark, he whispered, "It's too early to eat. I am not hungry. You get your rest."

"I'm worried about you, Love. You will not eat, and I do not think you sleep either."

He chuckled bitterly. "There's nothing to worry about. Who needs sleep? And I am

49

Wondering While Wandering

not hungry. Remember what I told you? Jesus called me a rock. Rocks are solid. They don't crumble to hunger."

She laughed as she rose and put her arms around him. "If I remember right, Master Rock, Jesus called you Cephas, which is not a rock but a mere chip from a stone."

In a daze, he repeated the words. "Mere chip from a stone? More like a pebble."

"Will you please try to sleep a bit longer? This past week has been daunting, and you need rest."

"Rest?" From deep within he groaned as he remembered Jesus in the Garden of Gethsemane asking him to watch and pray. He had tried, but sleep bogged him down pulling him deeply under. Rest. Jesus had wakened him, not once but twice asking him to watch and pray, and he? He had slept. When it was too late, Jesus, his master, his friend told him to sleep on. And...Now? Peter closed his eyes. He thought he may never sleep again.

He dragged his hands across his face. His shoulders sagged. He had failed. One thing Jesus had asked him to do, and he had failed. Just one thing, and that was to

Wondering While Wandering

pray to the God he loved to supply strength for the Master he adored.

Failure surged over him as he pulled away from his wife. "I have got to go."

She followed him to the door and touched his cheek. "Peter, Love, Jesus still loves you."

The man shuttered, turned, and walked away. He could feel her eyes on his back. He stopped. He wanted to hold her, but she deserved much better than he could offer. He kicked at the ground and sent a stone scampering ahead. He stooped and scooped it up, balancing it in his palm. He groaned. "A stone. Cephas, a stone." With a grip that ground the rough edges of the stone into his flesh, he pulled back his arm and threw the rock as far as it would go. He had no target, but he hit one, scattering a batch of squawking chickens. One old hen dropped from her roost, jerked, and lay dead. The stone had met its mark.

The rooster crowed.

Peter's world spun back in time. The cock crew. Again, through the crowd, the broken eyes of Jesus had found his.

Wondering While Wandering

Peter shook and glanced back at his wife. She clutched her throat. "I guess, Master Rock, there will be chicken for supper tonight." She smiled.

The fisherman's stomach retched. Would everything forever bring to memory his betrayal of his Saviour?

He shuttered, turned, and trod through the dark, dusty streets. His thoughts settled on the sop. They had all dipped the sop with Jesus, maybe not at the same time, but they all had shared the sop, and they had all betrayed him. It had not been for silver coins as Judas, but they had betrayed his trust. Peter clenched his hands and beat his chest. Oh, how he remembered what he wished he could forget. With pride, he had pledged to stand by Jesus even if his life were to be taken. Yet, before the cock crew three times, he, the fisherman, the rock, the stone, the pebble had crumbled. He had denied Jesus three times. Worse. He had denied his Lord and Saviour with a curse. The law had been drilled into his heart from childhood: 'Thou shalt not take the name of the LORD thy God in vain; for the LORD will not hold him guiltless that taketh his name in vain.'

Guilt, like thick gravy, pushed through the fisherman's veins. He was not guiltless.

Wondering While Wandering

His sin was great. Death was inevitable, and he wished it would come, except when it did, he would have to face his Saviour whose eyes dug deep into his heart.

Peter looked up. His feet had taken him to the shelter by the sea. A dim light flickered, so some of the disciples were gathered. His heartbeat quickened. Maybe Jesus would be there. Jesus had risen from the dead just like he had told them. Twice, Jesus had appeared in their midst from nowhere. The disciples hid behind closed doors as wanted men. What was to become of them? Before that horrible day, they had walked the streets boldly; now, in secret, they closed and locked doors and shuttered at shadows.

This was all wrong. Jesus had not been here to establish his kingdom. He had not stayed with them after he conquered death, and he was not going to stay.

Ahead, a hush settled over the group of men, and the fisherman heard someone say, "Quick. The fire."

Peter stepped into the group. "Worry not about the fire. It is I."

Relief spread.

Wondering While Wandering

With a glance, Peter's eyes scanned the group. His shoulders fell. Jesus was not among them. The fisherman sat, but he was restless.

Talk around the fire was the same. Judas had betrayed Jesus for money, thirty pieces of silver. Who could have known? They all trusted Judas. How could they have stopped what they did not know? How? Now Judas was dead, and Peter was glad.

The fisherman swallowed. He knew about Judas's betrayal, and he accepted it. But he, Peter, the stone, was no better than Judas. For fear he had betrayed his Lord and Master. He was glad he was away from the fire as the dam in his heart gave way to a torrent of tears he could no longer hold back. He choked as he remembered. Oh, he had been so bold. He had swung the sword which sliced off the ear of one who came to take Jesus away! But did Jesus thank him? No. Jesus put the man's ear back on his head and told Peter to put up his sword. What did the Saviour want?

The Stone shook his head. He did not know what to do. Life would never be the same. Jesus had touched him in so many ways, and now he did not know if he could live without his Lord...and worse yet, he did not know if the Lord wanted him any longer. He, Peter, the rock, the stone was broken, and he needed fixed, healed.

The rugged fisherman stood and faced the spray of the sea. He narrowed his eyes. He had walked on that very water with Jesus.

Nathaniel broke into his thoughts. "Peter, what are you going to do?"

Peter threw his hands in the air and shrugged. "I go a fishing." He trudged toward the water. He knew how to fish. He did not know how to follow a master who was not by his side.

The wind spewed water over him. The sea was far from calm, but not wild. Stars splattered the sky, and even though it would be a late start for a night of fishing, it should mount to a good catch.

The sea. Jesus had used their own fishing vessel as a platform to preach to the multitudes.

His master had sent him to these shores to catch a fish and pull a coin from its mouth to pay their taxes.

On his ship in the middle of the raging storm Jesus had slept. How could Jesus have been so calm? Peter remembered waking him to save them from the miry depths of the sea, and all the Master had said was, "Peace be still."

Wind and waves obeyed his voice!

There was no question in Peter's heart, but that Jesus truly was the Son of God. Yet something was wrong. Before the crucifixion he and the other disciples were with Jesus constantly. Since his Master had risen from the dead, Jesus had appeared only to vanish away. Peter groaned. His heart stopped. What if he never walked with Jesus on this earth again?

The short night was long. John stepped close to interrupt his thoughts. "Peter, it has been hours, and we have caught nothing. The sun is coming up."

The empty fisherman sighed. Another night wasted. Oh, there were plenty of fish in the sea, and they were still in the sea. He nodded, "Head for shore."

The fisherman wiped the salty mist from his face. Was he good at nothing? Always he had caught fish and been known as a good fisherman. Now? Nothing. His nets were as empty as his heart.

From the shore, a clear voice called, "Children, have ye any meat?"

Wondering While Wandering

Peter's shoulders sank. "No."

The stranger cupped his hand to his mouth. "Cast the net on the right side of the ship, and ye shall find."

Peter narrowed his eyes, searching the mist for the voice. What could this man know that they, the fishermen, did not know? There had been hours of work for nothing. There were no fish to be caught. Yet, what could they lose? Peter turned to his crew. "Cast the nets on the other side, men."

The men groaned but threw the nets into the water and watched them sink to the bottom. The water stirred. Shouts exploded, and all hands grabbed the nets. The boat tilted. Another vessel sped to their aid.

John clutched Peter's arm and gasped, "Peter, it is the Lord."

Peter dropped the net he held as his heart pounded. Only one could know such a thing as where the fish were. John was right. It had to be Jesus. Peter girt his coat about him. Then the Rock, the Stone, Peter cast himself into the waters and thrashed his way to his Saviour.

Wondering While Wandering

This time, he did not question if it was his Lord. He did not wait for Jesus to say, "Come." He had to get to his Lord and master. The others could bring in the boats.

Dripping wet, Peter ran to the fire, seeking the warmth of his Saviour. On the coals lay fish a plenty, and bread.

Peter stopped.

Jesus did not need their fish. The Master had spoken fish into existence! Peter swallowed. What lesson was he learning right now? Jesus did not need their fish. Jesus did not need them?

The Lord looked deep into Peter's eyes. "Bring of the fish which now ye have caught."

Peter nodded and trudged to the edge of the water. With fists tight and muscles bulging, he and his fellow fishermen dragged the swollen net of fish to the shore. In awe, he watched as the count was made. One hundred and fifty-three great fish. He gasped. They had dredged the waters most of the night with nothing to show for their work. Yet, the moment their net dipped into the sea at the command of the Lord, their nets were full to the breaking. He turned his eyes to his Saviour and whispered, "We had none, but you made our nets bulge." Was that what the Saviour was teaching? In the Lord's hands, whatever we have will be blessed mightily.

"Come and dine," Jesus welcomed.

They sat around the hot coals, feasting on fish and fellowship with their Saviour. Words were not needed. The Lord was with them.

After their bellies were full, Jesus broke the silence. "Simon, son of Jonas, lovest thou me more than these?"

Peter's eyes traveled over the boats, the nets, and the fish bones strewn on the sand. These fish were the biggest catch he had made since he first met the Saviour. He gazed at these men, his brothers in Christ. Again, his eyes rested at the feet of Jesus... whom he had betrayed. "Yea, Lord, thou knowest that I love thee."

"Feed my lambs."

Peter swallowed a bitter lump. His memory crashed into the judgment hall and the damsel that kept the door of the high priest. She had asked him, "Art thou also one of this man's disciples?"

His heart pounded with the memory of his own bold words. "I am not." Those words were the words that woke him in the dead of the night, and Jesus knew. Jesus knew he had denied him.

Again, Jesus asked, "Simon, son of Jonas, lovest thou me?"

This time Peter's eyes dare not stray to the nets or his friends. Wounded, they touched the gaze of the Saviour, "Yea. Lord, thou knowest that I love thee."

"Feed my sheep."

Peter studied his own rough, fisherman hands before they settled on the raw nail scarred hands of Jesus. There was no comparison. His betrayal haunted him. Guilt swept through Peter. His stomach churned as he remembered the fear. He recalled the kinsman of the man whose ear he had cut off. That kinsman had asked Peter if he knew Jesus. Peter shuttered and shook his head. Oh, he had been the Rock, so valiantly trying to save the life of his Lord. Wildly, he had swung his weapon and sliced away the man's ear. Peter grimaced. The ear was not what he had been aiming for. He had wanted his head. Peter closed his eyes. But what could one expect? He was a fisherman not a swordsman. Yet, what crushed his heart even more was that the Saviour did not

Wondering While Wandering

want to fight the soldiers. He had reached
out and gently put the ear back on the man.
Then Jesus had walked with those men
willingly! Peter swallowed. When the
kinsman of the man Peter had sliced the ear
from asked if he had been with Jesus,
terror had filled Peter. He had denied
knowing Jesus, and he had done it with a
curse. Immediately the cock had announced
his denial to the world.

A curse. "Thou shalt not take the
name of the LORD thy God in vain; for the
LORD will not hold him guiltless that taketh
his name in vain."

Peter was not guiltless, and he knew
it. He was not worthy of the Lord. Feed his
sheep? How could Jesus possibly want to
use him to feed his sheep? He who had
betrayed his Lord, not once, not twice but
three times! How could the Lord trust him
with his flock? Peter's eyes blurred. "Yea,
Lord, thou knowest that I love thee."
Ringing through his head were the words,
"And thou knowest what a sinful traitor I
am."

As if Peter and Jesus were the only
ones on the shore, Jesus asked again,
"Simon, son of Jonas, lovest thou me?"

Wondering While Wandering

The grief, the heartache, the pain, the burden Peter carried tormented him. Each time his master asked if he loved him, Peter vividly thought of his denials. Would he ever be free of the burden of his sin? He lifted his eyes to Jesus, and peace flooded his soul. Could it be that Jesus would forgive and use a traitor like him, a sinner? Peter gasped. Jesus knew the deep, dark crevasses of his heart, where his sin dwelled, and still Jesus would ask him to feed his sheep? Peter would jump at the chance to serve his master. "Lord, thou knowest all things; thou knowest that I love thee."

With a touch of a smile and the nod of the head Jesus answered, "Feed my sheep."

For the first time, Peter knew what it was to be truly forgiven. His battle had not been fought with the sword but with self. Hanging on to Jesus as Master, Peter had won the war within and felt life flowing through his soul. This was that life. The forgiveness of Jesus flowing through him brought life to Peter, Cephas, the Stone,

I Peter 2:5

"To whom coming, as unto a living stone, disallowed indeed of men, but chosen

Wondering While Wandering

of God, and precious, Ye also, as lively stones, are built up a spiritual house, an holy priesthood, to offer up spiritual sacrifices, acceptable to God by Jesus Christ."

Peter, the stone, a chip off the Rock preached to thousands on the day of Pentecost. Three thousand were saved. When we are saved, the Holy Spirit dwells within us making us lively stones. Just think what we could do if we let the Holy Spirit lead in our life!

"Lovest thou me? Feed my sheep."

Wondering While Wandering

Jochebed
Exodus 2

"She considereth a field, and buyeth it: with the fruit of her hands she planteth a vineyard." Proverbs 31:16

She looked down into the face of her baby boy. She knew every feature by heart. She had prayed for him from the moment she had an inkling she carried a babe in her womb. She had prayed he would be a girl child, but God had not listened.

She swallowed and wiped a betraying tear from her cheek. "Shhh, shhh...my little one," she crooned as her baby's voice quivered and bolted into a mighty wail. "Oh, my healthy man-child you cannot cry." One last time she cuddled him to her breast and watched the door for soldiers that might have heard and come bursting into her home. Silence. All was well. Again, Abba had blessed, but how much longer would it be before her son was found out, yanked from her arms, and thrown into the river? She had seen the soldiers at work. They all had. She shuttered. These were troubled times!

Wondering While Wandering

She looked again into the face of her baby, and her heart sank. She could not keep the secret of his presence any longer. Someone would hear his cry in the night. Someone would question Aaron or Miriam, and they were too young to keep silent. Or someone would find out and think it was not fair their baby had been thrown into the river and hers had not. Her own people would turn her in because she was breaking the law and making it harder for them to be the slaves they were. But worst of all, she had watched her husband refuse to hold and love their son, and she knew it was his fear of being found out, having their baby torn from their hands and hurled into that river.

She closed her eyes and heaved a heartbroken groan. It was time. Really it was past time...but she had been preparing for this time.

Over her shoulder, she motioned for her older children. "Aaron, go watch the path to the river. Do not tell anyone what you are doing; just watch the way and let me know when there are no soldiers."

Aaron nodded and turned to run outside and across the sand. "Miriam, bring me the basket we finished last week."

Wondering While Wandering

Miriam, too, obeyed without a question. They knew their Mether well, and asking why was not an option.

She gazed into the face of her babe and gently patted away one of her fallen tears. She rocked her baby boy until he sank into a deep sleep. Then she swaddled him tightly. She brushed his cheek with her lips and gently laid him in the basket she had prepared for him with rushes from the river's brink. She had pitched the basket with slime from the very river that had swallowed up so many boy babes. She knew there would be no leaks. She had tested the basket. The cargo this basket would carry was precious.

She whispered, "Abba, this is the son you have given me. I begged you for a girl. I pleaded for a girl so I would not have to fear for the life of my child." The young mother swallowed a sob. "But he is your will, your miracle, Abba, and I love him and thank you for him."

She closed her eyes, and tears streamed. She swallowed. "Abba, he has grown faster than I wished, and I have no safe place for him." She looked up to the roof. "Abba, I must place him in your hands for safekeeping. This basket, Abba, is like the ark you saved Noah and his family in. It is made of bulrushes from that river of death, but it is prepared just like that ark. I pitched and waterproofed it against the very waters my baby boy was to be thrown into the day he was born. Abba, I have hidden him for three months, and I cannot hide him any longer. He is too strong and too healthy a boy." Her heart built into a rapid pounding. "I am going to cradle him inside this basket and place him in that wicked river that has claimed the lives of so many of our baby boys, but, Abba, I have prepared him to survive those treacherous waters. Not a day has gone by that I have not fought the enemy for him and begged you, Abba, to watch over him and use him in your mighty plan."

She didn't even know her tears were streaming.

Aaron breathed from the door. "Mether, the way is clear. No soldiers."

"Thank you, Son." She choked as she motioned for her daughter.

Miriam slipped beside her with the top to the basket. The little girl did not say a word, but her cheeks glistened with tears.

Wondering While Wandering

"Thank you, Miriam," her mother whispered as she took the lid and lashed it to the top of the basket.

Still, her baby boy slept.

When the basket was firm, she leaned over and touched her lips to the reeds. Then she turned to her daughter. "Listen to me, Miriam. I want you to take your baby brother to the brink of the water, place the basket into the reeds and push it out into the river."

The little girl looked at her mother with horror. "Mether, there are crocodiles!"

Her mother placed a warning finger on her daughter's lips to silence her. "Yes, Miriam, yes, there are crocodiles," she closed her eyes and swallowed before she continued, "but we must believe Abba is stronger than the crocodiles. Our Abba will watch over him."

Wide-eyed, the little girl nodded.

The mother stood, placed the basket in her daughter's arms, and turned her to face the door, "Now, Honey, go and do as I say."

Sobbing, the little girl asked no more questions. She tightened her arms about

Wondering While Wandering

the bundle and carried her burden away from the house toward the river.

Their mama stood at the door. She dared not blur her vision with a flood of tears but watched until her daughter and the basket with her precious cargo disappeared into the tall flags by the river.

Aaron slipped his hand into hers and clung tightly. "Mether, will we see him again?"

She clutched her throat with one hand and held tightly to her son's hand with the other. "Aaron, baby, I do not know, but I must believe Abba has a plan for your little brother. I do not know what it is, but Abba must have a plan."

Time stood still as she went about her morning chores, and always as she passed the door, she looked to the river. A prayer tumbled from her heart and tripped over her lips. Aaron clung to her side, his wide eyes watching her every move.

"Mether! Mether! Come fast, Mether!"

She dropped the water pot. It shattered and spread water across the sand of the doorway. She stood still, yet her heart raced.

Wondering While Wandering

"Mether!" From across the sand, a little girl called. "Mether!" She knew it was her daughter. She would know Miriam's voice anywhere, and something was wrong.

Aaron grabbed her hand. "Mether? It's Miriam, and she doesn't have the basket." He whimpered. "Is he gone?"

She scooped up her toddler and held him close. "I don't know," she whispered as fear choked her heart.

Miriam was out of breath. She stopped at the door and clung to the frame, "Mether!"

"Miriam?"

"You must come quick!" Miriam gasped. "Pharoah's daughter found the basket!"

"No! No!" She sank to the ground and buried her head in Aaron's chest. Pharoah's daughter had found her baby boy. That was it then. He was dead. She looked to the sky and accused, "Abba, I put him in your care!" She wailed.

Miriam pushed Aaron away and grabbed her mother's shoulders with laughter. "Mether, Mether, the Pharoah's daughter, did not kill him. She did not throw him into the river! She wants to keep him and raise him as her own."

71

Wondering While Wandering

"But...but he is Hebrew," she whispered. "Does she know that?"

"Yes, she knows he is Hebrew, and she does not care. Her maidens told her he was Hebrew, and do you know what she said to them?"

"No," she breathed.

"The Pharoah's daughter said, 'He is a baby. He does not know he is Hebrew. Is there anyone here who will tell him he is Hebrew?' And all the maidens shook their heads, but they told her that the Pharoah, her father, would know the baby was Hebrew, and he would order the baby to be thrown into the river."

Miriam giggled, threw her hands in the air, and swirled in a circle. "Do you know what the Pharoah's daughter said to that?

With hope, Mether shook her head and held her breath.

Miriam bubbled. "The Pharoah's daughter laughed and bragged, 'The Pharoah? My father? I can talk my father into anything I ask." And they all thought that was funny. But their laughing caused our baby brother to cry. He was sobbing and bellowing really loud, so I took a big breath, and I walked right up to the princess, and I asked if she wanted me to go find someone to nurse that baby. Pharoah's daughter said, 'Go! Go!' So, I am here to take you to nurse our baby brother."

"The Pharoah's daughter wants me to come nurse him?"

"Yes. And if you listen, you can hear him bawling from here. We had best hurry before Pharoah's daughter changes her mind!" Miriam tugged on her hand to help her from the ground.

She stood. She brushed the tears from her face and the sand from her skirts. She raised her eyes to heaven. "Abba, mighty Abba, worker of miracles, thank you, Abba." Then she raised her skirts and ran to the river.

****

Centuries later, we know this mama to have been Jochobed. She knew her child was placed in her hands by God himself in the midst of troubled times. Jochobed was not even the one who named her son Moses, and what she called him was never recorded. The Pharoah's daughter named him. Jochobed didn't know what God's plan

Wondering While Wandering

for her son would be, but she was given a few short years to nurture him, and in that precious time, she taught him who he was, who his people were, and most of all: whom God needed to be in his life. Her teaching was so vital Moses could not forget it in years to come.

In Proverbs 31:16 "She considereth a field, and buyeth it: with the fruit of her hands she planteth a vineyard."

Jochobed considered her children to be a field. She purchased that field at mighty cost. With the fruit of her hands, (her children) she planted a vineyard.

We can only imagine the taste of the wine from the fruit of that vineyard.

Mama's, Jochobed is a heroine from God's Word. You can be, too. Consider your children to be a field. Purchase that field and plant a vineyard for the Lord.

74

Wondering While Wandering

Living Water

John 4

Quietly Miriam slipped inside and closed the door behind her. She leaned against the cold wood with dread. Soon that group of men gathered about the well would leave. She hoped. They must have more important things to do than stand around and talk or gossip. Miriam closed her eyes and pulled in a deep breath. She could not afford to be the object of their gossip, yet she could not put off getting water much longer. She crossed to the table and sat to wait. Sunshine from the window spackled the tabletop and made the thin film in the bottom of the water pot dance. She studied her reflection in that tiny pool of water. Gently she eased her hand to her swollen cheek. Already her left eye opened but a slit, and it was shadowed in deep blues and shades of purple.

A burly man bulged through the bedroom and leaned against the door frame. "Miriam? You got that water heated up yet? Woman?" his sleepy, gravelly voice demanded.

Wondering While Wandering

"Not yet," quietly she answered.

"Not yet?" he parroted. "I sent you ages ago. You're about as useless as a dead dog."

"I am sorry, Malcom," Miriam dropped her eyes to the dirt floor.

On bare feet he tromped to her side, his big shadow falling over her, making her shiver. She was not cold, but her blood was.

She tensed as he raised his hand to strike. In a flash, she grabbed the water pot, ducked beneath his arm and flew out the front door trying to slam it behind her.

He busted the door wide smashing it against the side of the house letting his form fill the doorway as his shout polluted the air. "Good for nothing swine. That's all you are. Good for nothing swine!"

Miriam dared to glance back and was relieved to find he was the only thing planted in the dried ground before the house. Even though he did not move, he continued yelling horrid names after her and finally ended by spitting into the dust at his feet. A dog scooted for shelter behind the wall. People all around stopped to stare, and chickens scattered.

Miriam turned back to the dirt track in front of her and slowed her pace to study the well: her destination. Finally, most of the men were leaving the well and heading down the path, but it was toward her. She looked at the ground and pulled her head cloak to drape over her swollen face. The men seemed unaware she existed, and she was glad. To further her fading into oblivion, she stepped off the thin road and let them pass before she continued. A couple of the men looked her way, but they seemed only concerned about the city before them and finding something to eat.

Ahead, Miriam watched the well and paused. One man remained. He did not seem to have anything to draw water with, and she hoped he would leave. But...it looked like she was to have no such luck. He sat on the rock wall of the well. She sighed. Miriam tried never to come to the well when anyone was there. She knew who she was and what she was, and she knew how people felt about her. They called her names. Mothers steered their children away from her. Men jeered and smirked at her. Miriam knew

Wondering While Wandering

Malcom, the man at home, was right. She was as a swine. She was filth, deplorable filth. She had no hope.

The lone man was still sitting on the edge of the well. Miriam slowed her pace. Still, he did not look to be going anywhere, and she could not go back to the house without water. Malcom would teach her another 'lesson', and she had no other place to go.

Miriam decided she would just refuse to look at the man, pull water and get home as fast as she could.

She stepped to the well. To her dread the man spoke to her, "Give me something to drink."

She raised her eyes to his. He was not from Samaria, so maybe he did not know about her. He could not know what she was guilty of, only that she was a Samaritan. She could tell he was a Jew, and Jews hated her people. Miriam was surprised he even spoke to her. She narrowed her eyes and asked, "You know that I am a Samaritan, and you are a Jew. Jews have nothing to do with us, so why are you asking water from me?"

Wondering While Wandering

The man did not even answer her question but waved it aside. "If you knew the gift of God, and whom it was that asked a drink from you, you would have asked of me living water."

She took a quick step away from him, narrowed her eyes and studied him. "Sir, you don't have anything to draw water with, and this well is deep. So where are you getting living water? Are you greater than our father Jacob, which gave us this well? He drank here and his children and his cattle. Are you greater than he?"

She noticed a twinkle in his kind eyes as he answered. His hand swept over the mouth of the well, "If you drink from this well, you will thirst again. If you drink of the water I give," he pointed to his chest, "it will be a well of water spring up into everlasting life."

Miriam paused. If this were true, she would never have to come draw water at this well again. She would not have to wade through the people, her accusers, and all the embarrassment and hurt could be avoided. She hesitated only a moment, "Sir, give me this water, so that I won't thirst, and I will never have to come back to this well again."

The man paused, and Miriam felt that his eyes not only studied her bruised face but explored her battered heart. From out of the blue, he told her, "Go get your husband."

Her eyes grew big, "I have no husband."

He nodded, "That is true, Miriam. You have had five husbands, and the man you now live with is not your husband."

She stepped back and dropped the pot she carried. It did not shatter into pieces. It was her heart that exploded in her chest wildly pumping blood through her whole being. This was why she never came to the well when someone else was there. It was the very thing she had been trying to hide. And he knew it. He knew her name, and he knew what she had done. This man knew her and had come to throw her sin in her face. She shrunk from the truth, dropped her glazed eyes to the ground and covered her heart with her trembling hand. Adultery. Adultery. Adultery, and he knew it. The word surged through her veins. It meant death. Her death. Death. She ground her knuckles against her teeth. It was the most horrid death. Miriam had seen it before, so she knew what would happen. She would be dragged outside of the city limits, surrounded by her accusers as a pack of ravenous wolves. They would sling cutting remarks, sordid names, and finally they would close in to hurl stones and rocks until death claimed victory. Tears cascaded down her face as she pleaded to the God she did not know, "Please, please, Lord God, let the first rock find its mark that I might die quickly!"

In a fog of hope, Miriam closed her eyes and swallowed. There was a chance, one chance in a million, if she could change the subject maybe this accuser would forget her crime. To the man sitting before her she whispered, "I perceive that thou art a prophet. Our fathers worshipped in this mountain, but you say Jerusalem is the place where we are to worship."

Again, the hint of a smile played at his lips. The man spoke, "Miriam, believe me, the hour cometh, when ye shall neither in this mountain, nor yet at Jerusalem, worship the Father. Ye worship ye know not what: we know what we worship: for salvation is of the Jews. But the hour cometh, and now is, when the true worshippers shall worship the Father in spirit and in truth: for the Father seeketh such to worship him. Miriam, God is a Spirit: and they that worship him must worship him in spirit and in truth."

Miriam gulped. She forgot her fear of this man and eased nearer. In excitement she spoke, "I know that the Messiah is coming, and he will be called Christ and he will tell us all things."

The man looked deeply into her eyes and nodded, "I that speak unto thee am he."

She threw her hand over her mouth and stepped closer to search his eyes. She wanted to ask more, but that group of men, the whole group, was back. They looked at her with disgust and disbelief that this man would talk with her, a Samaritan. Miriam was used to this, but she was drawn to the man. Again, she looked at him, and she knew this was the Christ. She had found the Christ, the promised Messiah. She gasped, he had not condemned her to the death she deserved! He had offered her living water. Miriam had a hope she had never felt before. With this Christ, she could change. She turned and ran. There were others who needed to meet this Christ, and she had to hurry. They must know him while he tarried at the well. She wildly searched the streets and begged those she found to come meet a man who told me all things. "He is Christ, the Messiah! He knows me, and I know he forgives and loves! You must come!" she shouted through the streets and alleys. "Come to Jacob's Well!" And this time, Miriam didn't care how many people saw her at the well. She had hope. She had tasted the living water, and she would never thirst again! She was a new person, changed. Christ did not condemn her. How could they?

Miriam laughed. She could not remember the last time she had laughed, but this Living Water bubbled up inside her and spilled over. She turned to hurry the crowd that followed her to find the Christ, the Messiah! The giver of living water.

Wondering While Wandering

Wondering While Wandering

Naaman

II Kings 5

Noah dipped her hand in the lily pool outside the palace of Benhadad, King of Syria. As the water stilled, she studied her reflection. Years had passed since she had come here, but Jehovah God had watched over her. She marveled that she was safe in the very camp of the enemy. Yet, why was she here? Mether had taught her that the steps of a good man are ordered by the Lord, and the Lord delighteth in his ways. That meant she must remember the Lord in everything she did so the promise of God's delight would dance over her life. She thumped the water and giggled, watching her face wriggle over the pool. Then she sobered. Mether had stepped according to the Lord, but Mether was dead.

Noah's thoughts sunk back in time, a terrible time, a time of war. The sky was gray with the breaking of dawn. Noah could feel the tension in the air, and she could still smell the fresh dirt.

"Noah, listen to me. Whatever happens, you stay in this hiding place and do not make a sound. No matter what you hear, do not come out of this hole." Mether held her hands tightly on Noah's shoulders, her eyes never wavering.

"But Mether, it's dirty and crumbly and damp. And I know there are spiders and scorpions and bugs."

"I do not care, Noah. It's the only safe place for you to hide. This is serious. This could mean your life. You must listen to me! As bad as you think it is in this hole, it will be worse out there," She pointed toward the small opening. "This is war, and war is ugly and brutal."

A scream cut through the air severing all thoughts.

Noah shivered.

Mether pushed Noah back into the hole and jammed brush into the opening to hide the entrance. Then she turned and ran.

Noah buried her head in the dirt. This was her family's piece of Israel. But this was war. If they beat the Syrians her family would keep their land. If they lost, their land would be gone.

Noah placed her hand against the damp dirt and felt her heartbeat, or maybe it was the earth's heart beating.

Wondering While Wandering

If they won? If they lost? That 'if' was a big word. The Syrians had been encamped about their city for three days. Now they were on the move. The marching and the chanting ate at her nerves spurring trimmers through her body. Her heart was drumming in her ears. She licked her dusty lips, and the taste of rain filled her mouth. She loved the smell of wet dirt. It was Israel's dirt, her home, her land. The Syrians had no right to it, and she would be glad when they scooted home with their tails between their legs like the dogs they were.

Noah opened her eyes, inched toward the opening, and spread the branches of the brush to peek but a little. Mether should be coming.

The clashing, crashing, and clanking of metal told the young girl the battle had started. The yelling and shrieks of horror reverberated through the air. A young soldier ran into the clearing with a bloody sword. He dropped to his hands and knees, retching.

Noah trembled. Her abba was out there fighting in this battle. She slapped her eyes tight and prayed to her heavenly Father above. "Please, please bring my abba home safe, and help Mether get back to our hiding place."

A scream shredded the air. Noah's eyes flew wide. Her heart thundered in her chest, and the ground shook. That scream...That scream was Mether. That had to be Mether.

Noah held her breath.

Mether ran wildly through the clearing, her garments sailing behind. An enemy soldier followed in her wake. He reached out and grabbed her skirts, yanking her to the ground. "I told you not to run, but you would not listen to me! Now, Woman, you are my spoils of war!" His eyes leered with evil as they traveled over her.

Noah did not think. She had to save her Mether. She burst through the brush and ran. She grabbed up the sword from the young soldier and swung it into the back calf of the man standing over her Mether. She meant to hit much higher, but the sword was heavy, and she was a little girl.

He yowled. Blood splattered and poured from his leg. His face twisted in pain as he swung about, stumbling to meet the young girl.

"NO!" Mether yelled. "Run! Noah, Run!"

Wondering While Wandering

"That's my Mether!" Noah tightly clutched the sword and aimed it to slash again.

"Is it now?" The hardened soldier grinned.

Mether gasped, "Run, Noah, run!" She stumbled to her feet, grabbing the soldier to drag him away from her daughter.

The burly man threw Mether aside and flung his sword, pinning her to the ground.

With horror Noah's weapon fell from her hands. "Mether!" She flew to her mother and dropped beside her.

Mether shoved something into Noah's hand and whispered, "Run, Noah, run. Jehovah, God be with you."

"Mether," Noah wailed. The sword was stuck all the way through her Mether, and Mether was fixed solidly to the ground.

"Run! Noah, run!" Mether's voice wavered.

"Mether?" Noah begged, "Mether!" Tears gushed. "Mether!"

Mether did not answer.

Wondering While Wandering

Mether's soft brown eyes were opened to the sky, searing deeply into Noah's memory forever.

A rough hand yanked Noah from her mother's body. He whipped her around and leered into her face. "I saw that. She gave you something, and I claim it." He pried open the little girl's fingers and twisted the prize from her. He dangled the gold medallion from its chain and whistled as the sun glinted from it. "Gold. Egyptian gold. Old, old Egyptian gold!" He laughed.

Noah kicked him in the leg she had sliced earlier, yanked Mether's treasure from his fingers, and ran.

"Eeeow!" the man bellowed. "When I get my hands on you..."

Noah chanced a glance behind and tripped over the young soldier whose life had ebbed away. She smashed to the ground.

The old, hardened soldier kicked the body of the young warrior aside, laughed, and swept up the girl in a grip that squeezed the breath from her. He glared into her eyes.

She yanked his helmet from his head and slammed it into his face.

Wondering While Wandering

Spewing filthy words, the soldier dropped the little girl. "I will teach you a lesson you will not forget!" He scooped her up and threw her over his shoulder.

A resounding voice cut through the fight. "That is enough, Soldier." It was a low-coiled voice, but it held the strength and power of a worthy strike.

The soldier slowly turned and stood as straight as his wounded leg would let him. "Captain."

"I might have known it was you, Bochima. A young girl? You should be ashamed. Put the girl down."

"But, Captain, she's my spoils of war."

"And the woman?" He nodded toward Noah's mother.

Bochima shrugged. "It was me or her."

Noah pounded his back and kicked. "You coward! You putrid coward! That is my Mether!"

"Put the girl down." The captain ordered.

The soldier dropped the girl in a heap on the battleground. "But, Captain, she's got my spoils."

Wondering While Wandering

Noah spat at the horrid soldier. "This is not your spoils." She held her fist high. "This is my inheritance. My Mether gave it to me when you killed her."

The captain's brows met over his nose in disgust as he studied his soldier. "It was her mother's?"

He furrowed his sweating brow and shrugged. "She don't need it no more."

The captain's jaw twitched. "The treasure belongs to the little one." He motioned to the trembling girl.

Bochima growled as he stared in hatred at the girl. "But Captain, she's the enemy."

"Enemy? A woman and a young girl? You have caused shame to our country." He paused. "Soldier, give the girl her inheritance which you call your 'spoils' and bury the woman."

The man spat and wiped the back of his hand across his mouth. "Yes, Sir." Then he handed the medallion to the girl and lashed out his hatred under his breath, "You just wait. Soon as Captain rides away, that trinket and you will be mine."

The captain's lips toyed with a smile. He crossed his forearms on his saddle and bent down to look the girl in the eye. "Young Lady, do you want to stay here, or would you like to come with me?"

The soldier gaped.

Noah stood tall and bowed. Dirt was caked on her cheeks with streaks where her tears had run. "If you allow, I will go with you, Captain."

The captain reached down from his horse and pulled Noah to sit behind his saddle.

The enemy soldier growled.

Noah sat like royalty and gave the man, the murderer, a victorious smile.

He grimaced and again spat on the ground.

Peace settled in the arms of the enemy. The captain asked questions, and Noah answered while holding on tight. The life she knew was gone, and what would become of her, she did not know. Only her heavenly Abba above knew the answers to questions that ran rampant in her mind.

Naaman brought Noah into his home courts to meet his wife with these words. "Noah has a touch of royal blood, I believe. She was a mighty bold young lady when I

Wondering While Wandering

found her. I would like to keep her as a maid in our home if you agree. I know you get lonely when I am gone, as we have no children."

With kind eyes, the woman looked her up and down.

Naaman nudged Noah toward the lady. "Show my wife your medallion."

Noah looked to the man, crossed to the lady, and held out the gold.

Naaman smiled. "The medallion came from Egypt, and I believe it has been passed down through the generations, all the way from The Great Exodus of the Jews."

Noah nodded. It was one of the things they had talked about on the journey.

"It is beautiful," his wife whispered.

"It is, and it belongs to Noah. I hope to petition King Benhadad to keep Noah as a maidservant in our courts. I pray that meets your approval, my Dear."

"Of course." She smiled, and it was beautiful.

The flutter in Noah's heart calmed.

Wondering While Wandering

That was how she had come to be in the enemy camp. She found Naaman was Captain of the Host of the King of Syria. He was a great man with his master and honourable because, by him, the Lord had given deliverance unto Syria: he was also a mighty man of valour.

The trumpets sounded far beyond her thoughts and memory, startling Noah and bringing her back to the present. She splashed the water of the pool one last time and stood. She knew those trumpets meant the army was coming back victorious. Her heart pounded. She had to run home and tell her mistress the master would soon be there. She needed to lay out her mistress's best attire, help her bathe, attend to dressing her, and braid her hair. The mistress always wanted to be her best for the master's return.

As she whirled to go, a young soldier stopped her. "Noah?"

"Yes?" She paused.

"A note for your mistress from the captain." He pressed a sealed paper into her hand.

She smiled, "Thank you. My Mistress will be very happy."

Wondering While Wandering

The young man dropped his eyes, and sorrow touched his smile.

Noah tipped her head with apprehension but quickly shoved those thoughts aside. The captain was home. Her mistress would be so delighted.

Noah ran. She threw open the door and called, "Mistress Eliel, the master is home. The trumpets are sounding!"

Mistress Eliel stood, dropping her sewing to the marble floor. "Noah, come help me. We must hurry."

"Wait," Noah's eyes lit with delight. "I have a note for you from the Master."

Her mistress laughed, "From the Master? Quick, Noah, give it to me."

Noah handed her the note, and her mistress tore the seal open. Her eyes ran down the page with eagerness changing to horror. "No." She whispered. "No, no, no. It cannot be." She wadded up the paper and drew her hands to her heart.

"Mistress Eliel? Is all well?"

"No. No, Noah, it is not well." She sank to the couch. "My Naaman is not coming home. He is never coming home again." Tears filled her eyes to overflowing.

Wondering While Wandering

Noah shivered. "He is dead?"

"He may as well be." Her shoulders sagged as she dropped the wadded note. "He has leprosy."

Noah's heart grew cold. Captain Naaman and Mistress Eliel had been her refuge. They had loved her as a coveted servant, maybe even as the child they had never been blessed with. She knew leprosy to be the kiss of death.

Gently Noah knelt before her mistress and placed her hand on her arm. "I know a man that can cure Master Naaman of his leprosy."

Mistress Eliel swung about. "Noah do not tease. There is no cure for leprosy. It is a death sentence."

Wildly Noah shook her head. "It does not have to be death. Would God my lord were with the prophet that is in Samaria! For he would recover him of his leprosy."

"Noah?"

The maid nodded. "It is so. The prophet is of our Lord God, Jehovah. He does miracles, and I know he would heal the captain."

Wondering While Wandering

Mistress Eliel grabbed the wadded note from the cold marble floor, stood, and spread the crinkles from the paper. "Then we will send the good news to my husband, the captain."

When the news of the cure came, King Benhadad looked at his Captain from across the court. Naaman was a good man, the best to be had. He trusted his troops and his country to this man. He was worth the cost of the cure. He called from his throne, "Go to, go, and I will send a letter to the King of Israel."

Within days, Captain Naaman was carrying a letter from King Benhadad to the King of Israel along with ten talents of silver, six thousand pieces of gold, and ten changes of raiment, and in his heart the hope of a cure.

For Noah and her mistress, the waiting began.

Mistress Eliel paced back and forth day in and day out.

Noah tried her best to get her Mistress to settle down. She tried to persuade her to eat. She had the musicians come to play for her.

Wondering While Wandering

"Mistress. I am worried for you. Please eat." Noah begged.

Mistress shook her head. "I have tried, but food makes me ill. Music will not let my thoughts travel anywhere but to my love. The only thing that calms me is when I listen to you pray to your Jehovah God."

Noah licked her lips. "Then I will pray, but, Mistress, you could pray to my Abba, my Jehovah God, too. You can request your very heart's desire, and Jehovah will listen."

"But, Noah, your Jehovah is not my god." Tears welled in her eyes.

Tenderly, Noah whispered, "He could be your God."

"What?" Mistress Eliel's eyes searched those of the little maid. "How? I am a foreigner to your god. I am not a Jew. How could your god be my god?"

"You ask. You just ask Him to be your God." Noah's eyes were alive with hope. Maybe this was why Jehovah God had allowed her steps to bring her to this foreign country, to a people she did not know and a people that did not know her God.

Mistress Eliel grabbed Noah's hand and looked to the ceiling as if to heaven

Wondering While Wandering

itself. "Noah's God, Jehovah, please, please be my God as you are Noah's God. Please help my unbelief to fade into the solid faith that Noah lives and breathes."

Trumpets sounded, breaking through her prayer. Shouts shook the walls. There was a banging at the door.

Noah ran and threw the door wide.

A soldier stood tall and announced, "The Captain is marching into the city."

"The captain?" Hope fired in her eyes.

"Yes. Captain Naaman." The soldier answered with a flicker of a smile.

Mistress Eliel grabbed Noah's hand. "My captain? Noah, oh, Noah, let's go see what our God has done!"

They raced through the streets and shoved among the people until they gasped for breath at the palace steps. The chariots rolled up, followed by Naaman's entourage. As his chariot slowed, Naaman's eyes fell upon his wife. He jumped from the rolling chariot. He took her in his arms, held her tightly, and swung her about. When he sat her down, he kissed her lightly.

She whisked her tears aside. "The Leprosy?"

Wondering While Wandering

Widely he smiled. "No Leprosy, Eliel. My Lord God Jehovah took that horrible death from me. Our little maid, Noah, was right. Her country has a true prophet of the only true living God."

Mistress Eliel laughed as she corrected her beloved, "Our Lord God, Jehovah."

Naaman tipped his head, "You know Him, Eliel? You know the Lord God Jehovah?"

Her lashes flashed, flooding her eyes with joy. "Our little maid, Noah, introduced me to her Jehovah, and now He is mine."

Naaman wheeled about looking for the little Jewish maid. When his gaze spied Noah, he whispered, "What a blessed day that was when God gave you to my wife and me." He reached into his pocket. "I have not forgotten you, Noah. I have something for you from your homeland." He tossed her a leather pouch.

Deftly she caught it. She knew what it was before she opened the bag. It smelled of the best perfume ever. Dirt. The dirt of her homeland. She held it to her nose and breathed in deeply. "Israel!" she whispered and pulled open the strings of the bag. A tear spattered in the dirt, releasing the aroma of rain. "Rain! Oh, the smell of rain from my homeland!" She hugged the bag to her heart, and she could hear Mether's voice, 'The steps of a good man are ordered by the Lord.'

Noah looked from Naaman to Mistress Eliel and knew why God had ordered her steps here, and she knew her Lord was delighted in her ways.

"The steps of a good man are ordered by the LORD: and he delighteth in his way." Psalm 37:23

Wondering While Wandering

Sweet Baby's Breath
Luke 1:38-44

The marketplace was busy as it always was in the early morning. People were fresh and ready to face a new day, and the place was buzzing. Women were buying what food they needed for the day's meals. People were talking, laughing, and haggling over prices, seeking the best bargain they could get.

Elizabeth smiled. As far as food needs, she had not many. She desired to see the people at the market. Her heart melted within as she gazed at the group of young mothers with babies. Laughter bubbled up inside as she watched those with toddlers clinging to their mother's skirts. She caught the eye of a little boy and engaged him in a game of peek-a-boo. This was why she came to the market each day. She inched in closer. It helped soothe the ache of her heart. Oh, she knew she was way too old to have a baby. Time. Time had been cruel to her as month after month had passed, dashing her hopes of a babe. The years had wrapped her yearnings into a package labeled 'Barren.'

Wondering While Wandering

She swallowed as she watched the young mother, Hadar, put one tired hand on her back to stretch while clutching a wiggling bundle of baby with her other arm. A toddler latched onto her leg and begged to be held. "No, Jeremiah. My hands are full. You must be a big boy. You have to be my helper now."

His bottom lip flopped out, dropping a rebellious, "No! No helper!"

His mother thumped him on the head.

Jeremiah dropped to the ground and squalled.

His mother blew her hair away from her forehead. Her shoulders sagged with exhaustion.

Elizabeth stepped in to rescue her. "Hadar, I would love to help. Could I hold the little one or take Jeremiah if he would let me? Then you would be free to finish your shopping."

Hadar dropped her eyes. "I am so tired, Elizabeth, and Jeremiah is cranky today. He had just gotten somewhat used to his little brother, and now," she patted her belly, "he was going to have another. He does not understand why I have no time for him." Love in her eyes poured over the son plopped at her feet, bawling and twisting her skirts.

Elizabeth smiled, "Then, if I held the little one, you and Jeremiah could have a pinch of time together. Maybe that would comfort him?"

"I do not know," she hesitated. "It would help, I am sure. Would you mind? With one little boy, it would not take me nearly as long to make my purchases, and this one," she smiled into the baby's face, "he is so close to sleep. Are you sure you wouldn't mind?" Hadar's eyes glimmered with hope.

"Hadar, I do not mind at all. I would cherish the time holding Samuel. That is his name?" Elizabeth glowed.

Hadar nodded and whispered, "Thank you so much, Elizabeth. I promise I will hurry."

Elizabeth smiled. "There is no need to hurry, Hadar. I will love every minute with your little one."

They found a bench beneath the shade of a fig tree, and Elizabeth reminded the young mother to take all the time she needed. Then she settled to coo and sing softly to baby Samuel. Gently, Elizabeth rocked, and she felt her heartbeat settle into a rhythm with the little babe. "Oh." She closed her eyes and leaned in closer to the baby. "What beautiful music we make," she whispered.

Her heart yearned that Abba had never blessed her with a baby, but holding this precious little one eased her longing. She smiled as the babe sunk deeply into sleep, and a tiny snore sifted through the air. His breath brushed her cheek, toying with the rain of a teardrop that had escaped her eye. "What sweet baby's breath. I do not think any aroma smells so delicious!"

Elizabeth closed her eyes. She needed to talk to Abba. She must ask forgiveness because she so coveted a baby and must not let her heart grow bitter toward Abba.

It was then the group of young mothers walked by and paused.

"Do you see that? Hadar has let Elizabeth watch her little one... again."

Elizabeth sighed. That had to be Ada's voice.

"Oh, I see very well, and look. She has dozed off holding Hadar's baby. That is not responsible. But then, Elizabeth does not know how to be a mother. She has never had a baby of her own."

Elizabeth froze; her eyes peeked but a little. She recognized the young woman. That was Priscilla.

"If you ask me, it is good that Abba did not bless her. Just think what could have happened to a child of hers."

One mother, Martha, came to Elizabeth's defense, "Well, maybe when she was young, she would not have fallen asleep holding a little one. Besides," her voice was gentle, "I have fallen asleep rocking my children many a time."

"But not in the marketplace. I think Abba knows who can be trusted with children and who had best not have any." The mama, Priscilla, shifted her gaze, searching for her own children. Her lips thinned as she spotted them. "Abagail and Amos, both of you get back here right now. You know you are to stay close to me. Wait until your father finds out." The two children giggled and ran on. Priscilla turned and pointed to Elizabeth, "I tell you, Abba did not trust her with children, and neither do I."

Elizabeth's heart shattered as bile rose up in her throat. Still, she pretended to be asleep as she held tightly to the precious life in her arms. She shut her lips tightly. The things that raced through her mind were things she would regret saying if she birthed them with life.

"Priscilla, you are wrong," Martha whispered. "Elizabeth is a godly woman."

"Godly? Really? Do you know what else I noticed about your godly woman, Elizabeth?" Priscilla paused, waiting for the invitation to continue.

All eyes were on Priscilla.

"Well, tell us," Ada begged.

"I noticed Elizabeth standing sideways." She raised her eyebrows. "And do you know what I saw?"

"How could we know what you saw, Priscilla? You may as well tell us." Martha's voice held disgust.

Prisilla tipped her head. "Elizabeth looks to be with child."

Martha narrowed her eyes. "Priscilla. That cannot be, and you know it. Elizabeth is far past the age of bearing children."

Prisilla's thin lips pressed together as she cleared her throat. "I know that. I think she is pretending to be with child.

Wondering While Wandering

Maybe she has wrapped padding about her so she will look the part of a mother-to-be."

"Or maybe, Priscilla, she has put on a few extra pounds. Sometimes that happens when you get older," Martha stood up for the gentle, godly woman they all knew and had been taught to respect. "And, Priscilla, maybe you had better check on the children Abba placed in your care. They are about three booths down and arguing with the butcher, and I see he has his knife raised high in the air."

Priscilla gasped, turned, and yelled, "Abigail and Amos! I told you to stay close to me."

Martha smiled as Priscilla stomped toward her children. Then she whispered to the other young mother beside her, "I am so glad Elizabeth was asleep. I would have hated for her to hear the things Priscilla accused her of."

The two turned and tip-toed away to not disturb Elizabeth and the sleeping baby she held.

Elizabeth shook. How could Priscilla think those things of her? She did not know why Abba had chosen the path she trod, but it was Abba's path for her. She knew it was not because Abba felt she was unworthy or that Abba did not love her. Abba was Jehovah God, her heavenly Father. He loved her, and she did not doubt it.

Yet as soon as Hadar claimed her little one, Elizabeth trod a silent path home, vowing not to come to the market again when young mothers were shopping. She wished she could share her heavy heart with Zacharias, but since he had returned from his service at the temple, he could not talk. He had been sweet and kind. He had drawn pictures in the dirt, looked to the sky, and danced about as if he were the happiest of men. Others said he had had a vision that had left him dumb. And...some said Jehovah God had judged him. Elizabeth frowned. What would Jehovah God judge him for?

Elizabeth stepped into her house, shut her door to the outside world, and leaned against it. She vowed she would not go out again. She would stay behind the safety of the closed doors of their home.

She looked down. Her hands dropped to rest on her belly. Like lightning, shivers shot through her body. So, someone had noticed she was with child. She had thought it herself. How far along, she did not know. The way of women had passed her years ago, and it was not until her belly gained in size and shaped as a babe that the nagging thought hounded her constantly. Was she with child? Hope pounded with her rapid heartbeat. Was this what the pictures Zacharias had drawn in the dirt meant? She had thought her husband was saying she was growing bigger and needed to lose weight. But possibly, he could have been drawing her as if she were with child. She gasped. Maybe that was why he had danced with joy?

She caressed her hands in warm circles about her belly and tingled with joy. Laughter exploded. A baby? A baby! After all those years of disappointment? Elizabeth looked up and whispered in praise, "Thus hath the Lord dealt with me in the days wherein he looked on me, to take away my reproach among men." She could not wait to go to the market with her own baby cuddled in her arms! She would certainly want to smile and maybe even wink at that young mother, Priscilla.

Elizabeth felt young, and happiness swept her in a dancing flurry about the room. Jehovah God loved and cared for her. Zacharias would be so elated. This baby would change their whole life. She stopped and put her hands to her cheeks. They were

Wondering While Wandering

warm, and she knew they glowed with the
promise of motherhood. She would fix
Zacharias's favorite meal tonight; then she
would share the miracle Abba had graced
them with. She grabbed sticks for the fire,
mixed bread, and seared meat. Time flew.
Zacharias came home, and the night was
wonderful. She would remember it forever.
The Lord God Jehovah had blessed them
beyond measure.

But as time passed, a nagging fear
chiseled through her joy. She gently
stroked her growing womb. She paused and
held her breath. Growing? She was growing,
but was the babe growing? What if she was
all that was getting bigger? What if there
was no baby? Her heart pounded in her ears
as fear exploded. Her hands dropped to her
sides. Five, maybe close to six months had
passed, and she had felt no movement.
Surely, she should be feeling movement.
She had thumped her belly. She had
massaged and pushed the babe about, but
there was not even a shutter of motion.
Nothing wavered. What if Jehovah God had
blessed her...but...the babe was to be
stillborn?

Slowly, Elizabeth collapsed in her
kitchen chair, her hands cradling her womb.
She eased to the edge, slipped from the

seat, and to the floor. On her knees, with the chair for her altar, she knelt to pray. No one could understand her but Jehovah God because her words were flooded with tears as she sobbed. Her heart split into a million pieces. In desperation, she whispered, "Please, Abba, please, breathe your breath of life into this sweet babe you trusted me to carry. Please, Abba, do not let me labor to bring forth a babe who has tasted death, never having tasted life..."

A rap on her door crashed through the intimacy of her precious time with her Lord.

Elizabeth sighed. Someone was knocking on her door? No one ever came to visit her anymore. And she was on the floor. Could she get up? She was old and heavy with child.

Whoever it was pounded on the door with impatience.

"I will be there. Give me a minute." Elizabeth called. She grabbed the chair with one hand and the edge of the table with the other. It took all her strength, but she pulled herself to a stand. She whisked her apron across her face to wipe the tears she had shed. Then she put a hand to her back and stretched. She smiled as she remembered Hadar doing the same at the market months ago. Now she knew why. This baby had taken a toll on her body. Slowly, she walked to the door, opened it wide, and gasped, "Mary? Mary! What are you doing here?"

"Elizabeth." That was all Mary said, and it was but a whisper. Yet it was the best thing Elizabeth had ever heard. Her babe, who she had never felt, not only moved but leaped in her womb! Elizabeth laughed, and Elizabeth cried. Elizabeth praised Jehovah, her Lord and God. He had heard and answered her prayer. She grabbed Mary and pulled her into a robust, tender hug.

"Mary, blessed art thou among women, and blessed is the fruit of thy womb. And whence is this to me, that the mother of my Lord should come to me? For, lo, as soon as the voice of thy salutation sounded in mine ears, the babe leaped in my womb for joy. And blessed is she that believed: for there shall be a performance of those things which were told her from the Lord."

Elizabeth looked to the Lord God above. "Jehovah God. Thank you!" Then she patted her tummy, and that baby kicked her hand, bolting it through the air with mighty strength!

Wondering While Wandering

"Life!" Elizabeth laughed. "Jehovah has answered my prayers. My babe has not only tasted life... he dances with it!"

Wondering While Wandering

Wondering While Wandering

The Carpenter

Matthew 1:18-25

He adored her. Her cheeks were full and rosy. Her damp hair clung to them, and her lashes splashed against her skin. In awe, he wondered how she could sleep after all they had been through. If the day had not been treacherous enough, the night had exploded with surprise after surprise, miracle after miracle. He could not even close his eyes for thought after thought raced through his memory. He looked about. The cow chewed her cud. A donkey softly brayed, and the sheep muttered in their sleep as if nothing extraordinary had happened.

Well, it had happened, and it was extraordinary! Mary had given birth to the Son of God. Angels had ripped the sky apart with singing, and shepherds had come knelt before the King of Kings.

His heart was bursting with fear and honor. How could he be a father to God's son? And he had no doubt this baby was the Son of God. He trembled thinking of when the angel of the Lord had appeared to him in a dream. He shook his head. He was just a carpenter. How was he to raise the Son of God?

The baby stirred.

He reached over to take the bundle from this beautiful woman God had given him.

Her eyes flashed wide.

He whispered, "Everything is fine. I was going to hold him for you while you sleep."

She smiled. "He is a beautiful miracle, isn't he, Joseph?"

Shivers ran through his body. "He certainly is."

When he took the baby from Mary, the babe threw his arms wide and cooed.

Joseph jumped.

Mary laughed. "Are you afraid of a little baby?"

Joseph shook his head, then bowed it low. "Yes. Mary, I am terrified. I am responsible to God for His son. I am not worthy, and how shall I know what to do?"

"Joseph, maybe that is why God chose you." Mary leaned in close. "God knows your heart. He knows you will seek his will and do whatever He asks you to do. You are the man God chose. He did not want someone who already thinks he knows what to do. That kind of man would probably have put me away because he would not have believed this baby is God's son."

Joseph flinched. "Oh, Mary, I almost was that man, but God sent an angel in a dream to tell me you were truly carrying the Son of God."

Mary gasped. Her eyes were big and then she sighed. "But Joseph you believed God rather than man. You are the man who God wanted to raise his son."

"But, Mary, a carpenter?"

"A man after God's heart."

The bundle in his arms rumbled.

Joseph pulled him from his chest to look into his eyes. "What do you want, Little One?"

The baby flayed his arms wide, hitting the side of the wooden manger. His face crumpled in tears.

Mary reached for her baby and gasped, "Joseph, his hand is bleeding."

Gently, Joseph placed the baby in her arms and examined his hand. "Let's see what you have done. A splinter." His fingers felt so clumsy as he coaxed the sliver of wood from the tiny hand. "Little One, I am a carpenter. You are going to be around a lot of wood, and splinters happen." Joseph brushed his lips against the tiny finger, and the babe grabbed his beard. Joseph laughed. "With God's help, I will do my best to be the abba you need, Little One."

As time flew by, Joseph thought on these things. His carpenter shop was often his sanctuary. He was building a larger table. The family was growing. Laughter from outside delighted him. The boys were playing. Jesus ran into the shop, chased by his little brother.

"Not in my shop, Boys! This is not a playhouse." Joseph held a wood chisel in his hands.

Jesus ran behind Joseph to hide from his brother. His brother spied him and, with a shout of victory, dashed his way.

Jesus ran. "Eeow!"

Joseph whipped around. Jesus was plopped in the sawdust, holding his foot.

"Barefoot?" Joseph shook his head. "Never come into the carpenter's shop without shoes. Boys, there are wood shavings and splinters and nails." He knelt beside his son. "Let's see what you have found, Little One."

Tenderly he picked up his son's foot. He took a deep breath, "A nail." He shook his head. "Close your eyes, take a deep breath, and count to ten."

The little boy did as he was told, and on three his abba pulled the nail from his foot. He held it in the air. "Son, nails will hurt you. They can cause you to be very sick and they can even cause death. Please wear shoes in the carpenter's shop, Little One."

The little boy nodded.

A few years later, Mary groaned as she pulled herself from the table. Her rounded tummy slowed her movements. She shoved her fingers through her hair. "Joseph, please take Jesus to the shop with you today. I have James taking a nap, which he badly needed; Joses is crawling all over the place, and this one," she patted her tummy, "this one is already throwing a tantrum."

Joseph laughed, "Alright, Little One, grab your shoes, and let's go make something."

Wondering While Wandering

"Yahoo!" He swung in a circle and raced for his shoes.

As they walked to the shop, Jesus slid his hand in Joseph's, "Abba, I want to make something for Mether."

Joseph tipped his head, smiled, and asked, "What did you have in mind?"

The little boy twisted his lips with thought. "I want to make something for her to put her feet on when she sits down. She gets so tired. And I think she could use it to step up higher when she is trying to get things from the top shelf in the kitchen. I watched Mether, and it is really hard for her with that baby she has in her tummy."

Joseph chuckled. "I am sure it is. Son, that is a great idea. I think we can do it today."

The aroma of sawdust met them at the door. Joseph loved the smell. It made him feel at home and full of peace.

"Let's go to the scrap wood bin and pick a piece. We will get some nails and a hammer. I want you to practice pounding them into the wood before we begin."

The smile that spread over the boy's face melted the heart of the man. He tipped his head. This was God's son, not his.

Wondering While Wandering

He had to tell himself this over and over again. Then, the miracle struck his heart and took his breath away. Every time he touched his son, he touched God. Talking to God was as easy as talking to his son. He turned from the boy. He did not want God's son to see him cry. "Lord God in heaven, help me to do right by our son!"

The little boy slipped to his father's side and wrapped his arms about him. "Mether says it is okay to cry 'cause God understands our hearts, and I found a piece of wood, so I am ready for the hammer and nails."

"Ready for the hammer and nails?" Joseph echoed, and a chill shrouded his body. What did that mean? He brushed his sleeve across his face to wipe the chill away and swallowed. "Then we had best get to work, Son."

Pounding in the carpenter's shop was like rain on a wooden roof. Always, it was warm and cozy...until...the little boy yowled.

Joseph dropped his saw and stepped to his son's side.

The boy was holding his finger and jumping in circles.

Wondering While Wandering

"Let me see the damage, Son." Joseph picked him up and held him close.

Slowly the boy let go of his finger and shoved it closer to his abba.

Joseph planted his lips in a grim line. The finger was already swollen and turning blue. He knew the blood was a pulsating pain with each heartbeat. "It looks to need Mether," Joseph sighed, kissing the finger. He did not know what to do, but he had seen Mary kiss little boy's wounds, and it seemed to help. Then, as a father, he explained. "Carpenter tools are dangerous, Son. They are made for good, but if used carelessly or wrongly, they can be very disastrous."

The boy nodded.

"Shall we go find Mether?"

The little boy shook his head. "Can I finish what I am going to make her first?"

"Do you feel like it, Son? Mether will understand."

His smile made his face glow. "But I want to do this for Mether to show her I love her."

Joseph swallowed. "Then we will finish this together for Mother."

Wondering While Wandering

The years swept by fast.

The road was hot and dusty, but what a blessed time they had had at Passover. A few days and they would be home.

Mary touched his arm, "Joseph, have you seen Jesus? All the other boys are here, but I cannot find hide nor hair of him."

"No," he scanned the crowd. "I have not seen him since we started this morning. Have you asked around?"

"I have asked everyone, but no one has seen him," Mary's eyes cradled worry.

Joseph's lips were in a grim line. "When we make camp, we will search. If he is not here," he held his hands in the air, "we will turn back to Jerusalem."

He was not there.

In Jerusalem, they searched all the places they knew the boys had played. He was not in any of them. Desperation sunk in his gut. He was in charge of God's Son, and he had lost him!

Three long days they rummaged through the city and found him not. Three long days Joseph ate nothing, and watched Mary grow drawn and sober. "Please, Abba," he prayed, "Your Son was in my care, and I have lost him. I know you know where he is. Please, I beg you, Jehovah, help me find him."

It was the crowd passing that gave him hope. A rugged man chuckled, "In the temple. All those doctors keep asking him questions, and they seem astounded by his answers."

"A little boy?" another asked.

"Yes, a little boy, maybe eleven or twelve at the most."

Joseph's heart pounded so loudly he thought Mary would hear it. He grabbed Mary's shoulders and swung her about. "It's Jesus. It must be him."

"The boy in the temple?" she asked.

"Yes. I know it is!" Joseph took her hand, and they ran.

Out of breath, they stopped at the door of the temple. It was their son, Jesus, and they were amazed. Boldly, he answered questions, and he answered them correctly.

Mary burst forth, "Son, why hast thou thus dealt with us? behold, thy father and I have sought thee sorrowing."

Wondering While Wandering

Calmly, Jesus answered, "How is it that ye sought me? wist ye not that I must be about my Father's business?"

Joseph did not understand, but many a time he thought on those words.

As his Son grew, the Son of God seemed to burst from within. More and more, Jesus was God's Son, and he was slipping from Joseph's fingers. Joseph's heart broke at the things Jesus said. He knew men. Their very leaders would reject Jesus as the promised Son of God, and how could he, Joseph, Jesus's earthly father, stand by and watch that rejection? What would they do to Jesus? He loved this Son whom God had placed in his hands. Would he be able to stand aside and watch how the world treated him? They expected him to be a carpenter's son, and he was. He could make anything with wood. Really, Jesus had surpassed all Joseph could teach him of wood.

Joseph smiled. Yes, he could make anything with wood. He was God's Son. Just think what he made with a pile of dirt! And what he had made with a rib!

Joseph sat with his elbows on his knees and his head in his hands. Fear struck like a bolt of lightning. What if the next thing God's Son made cost him his own blood?

Joseph sunk into the sawdust of his shop and sobbed. How could he face what was coming? He took his feelings, his broken heart, to God, his heavenly Father. After all, it was just like talking to his young son, who was not so little anymore. "Abba, Father, I do not know that I have the strength to watch all that man will do to your Son. You put him in my care; please, show me what I must do."

His Abba, God the Father, answered his prayer.

Joseph stepped into Paradise, and it was truly a place of peace. He was sitting at the door when Jesus, the son he had shared with God, crossed the threshold. A crown of thorns had slashed his flesh, and streams of blood had showered his face. His hands were ripped and gashed. His side was pierced, and his feet were gouged.

Aghast, Joseph shook his head and groaned. "Oh, Jesus, Jesus, my son, let's see what you have done this time."

A torn man beside Jesus answered. "I will tell you what He has done. They nailed Him on that cross right beside mine. In His agony, He forgave my sins and brought me with Him to paradise! Jesus is my Saviour!"

Joseph glowed. "That's my son! Always caring for someone else no matter what pain he was in." Joseph shook his head, and then he smiled. "Nails? You never took a liking to my carpenter's tools, did you, Son?"

Wondering While Wandering

Wondering While Wandering

The Perfect Lamb

Luke 2:8-20

Like a tiny finger from heaven, moonlight pointed to a little boy stroking the thick, dirty, oily wool of his very own ewe. He had cared for her just like his father had told him to do; only the chore of caring had turned into the blessing of love.

"Esther, it's going to be fine, I promise." The ewe kicked and bleated again as she lay on the scrubby grass.

The little boy tried to coax her to her feet, but she would not budge. He dropped to his knees beside his ewe. "Come on, Esther, I have to get you to my abba. He will know exactly what to do for you. I have never helped any sheep have a lamb before. He wrapped his arms firmly about the neck of Esther and tried to pull her to her feet.

Wildly, Esther protested.

The boy looked to the sky for help. "Abba, Father, please help me!" he wailed. "My abba knows what he is doing. I don't!" With the sleeve of his tunic, he raked unwanted tears from his face.

Esther bleated again.

The boy heard a stick snap and, with hope, called, "Abba?"

A low snarl from the brush made his blood run cold. He knew there were wolves roaming these hills, yet he had never faced them alone in the night. In one fluid motion, the little boy was on his feet with staff in hand, ready to swing and fight one wolf or the whole pack. That was what his abba had taught him to do, and he would try to do his best.

Esther struggled to her feet. She swayed and stumbled. She did not know what path to take. She did not know she should stay close to the little boy shepherd.

With horror, the little shepherd watched as she blindly crashed toward the scraggly brush where he knew the wolves prowled.

"NO! Esther, no!" he yelled and surged forward to save his ewe.

Esther leaped into the brush and was caught and wedged. She fought the thorny branches only to be more tangled and trapped in a grip that would mean cruel death to the ewe.

The little shepherd ran.

The wolf snarled and sprang toward his prey.

The boy jumped between the sheep and the wolf, yelled, and swung wildly with his staff. He smacked branches, the ground, and once his own foot before he felt the thud of a solid blow on the side of the attacker. The wolf yelped and backed away while Esther bleated louder, pleading for her life.

The little shepherd called over his shoulder, "You're on your own, Esther! My abba said I cannot take my eyes off the enemy!"

The wolf snarled.

The little boy shuttered and grabbed his staff with a tighter grip. The glowing eyes of the enemy followed the little boy. "Please, Abba," he whispered.

With a limp, the wolf began to circle the shepherd. The little boy kept himself between his ewe and the enemy. His eyes never fell from the blazing eyes of the wolf.

When the wolf pounced, the little shepherd held his staff ready, waited for the hot breath of the wolf, and then swung with strength he did not know he had. The weight of the enemy made the shepherd drop to his knees, but the blow of the staff sank the wolf to the ground. The wolf growled and snarled from deep within. The little shepherd exploded to his feet and plunged toward his enemy. As one, the boy with his staff became a weapon and pounded the life from the wolf.

The little shepherd's heart thudded. He shook and stood, clutching the staff. He let his eyes rove the darkness in search of other enemies before he turned to his ewe.

He was just in time to catch Esther's newborn lamb. He crooned to Esther, and with his cloak, he gently wiped and wrapped the tiny baby. From the tip of the lamb's nose to the end of his tail, the lamb was flawless...not one single spot blotted the lamb.

"Esther, your lamb is perfect!" he whispered in awe.

From the dark, a rich, deep voice called. "Joseph, Son?"

The little shepherd trembled, "Abba!" Joseph stood and held the bundle toward his abba. "Esther's lamb."

The little shepherd's father stepped over the dead wolf. "I see you had to fight for Esther and her lamb. It looks like you have done a man's work tonight."

"I did exactly what you told me to do, Abba. I never once took my eyes off the enemy, and I used the weapon you gave me and taught me to use. It was enough, just like you told me it would be."

"And did you watch for other enemies?" his father asked.

Joseph nodded.

His father smiled. "You have done a good job, Son. I am proud of you."

Joseph beamed. "Look, Abba. He is a perfect lamb." The little shepherd pushed the lamb toward his father.

His father nodded as he examined the lamb in his arms. "Perfect he is. Maybe he will be the sacrifice lamb for our Passover this year."

The little shepherd's heart lurched to a stop. Could he really have fought for the very life of this perfect, newborn lamb only to have him sacrificed?

"I am proud of you, Son," his father

handed back the lamb and rested his hand on Joseph's shoulder.

"But...Abba? The Passover lamb? It is not fair!" He held the newborn lamb in a tight grip to protect him.

His father searched his son's eyes. "No, Son. It is not fair. Someday, it will not be so. We will not have to sacrifice one of our lambs. God will give his own son to be our perfect lamb, and that? That is not fair, either. Innocence given for the guilty. Purity given for sinners. The King of Kings given for sinful mankind. No, Son, it is not fair, yet I look forward to the time."

In sorrow, the little shepherd stroked the tiny, perfect lamb. Then, he followed the gaze of his father's eyes. "Abba, isn't that the brightest star in all of heaven? Doesn't it look to be busting open the skies over Bethlehem? He gasped as his heart thumped faster, "Abba, do you hear singing?"

His father drew in a quick breath. "It is almost like the sound of Heaven," he whispered.

"Fear not."

The earth quivered. The sky burst open, and with his father, the boy fell to the ground.

"I bring you good tidings of great joy, which shall be to all people. For unto you is born this day in the city of David a Saviour, which is Christ the Lord. And this shall be a sign unto you; Ye shall find the babe wrapped in swaddling clothes, lying in a manger."

The little shepherd trembled. "Abba, can we go see?"

His father held him tightly. "Yes, oh yes, we can go see. I would not miss it for the world."

Gently, the little shepherd touched the tip of the lamb's nose. Greedily the little lamb latched a hold of his finger and began to suck. "Abba, can I give Him, the Saviour, my perfect lamb?"

"The Saviour?" With a deep breath and a touch of pain, his father spoke, "Son, do you realize you would have to give Esther, too? That little lamb needs his Mether, and they are all you have."

The little boy nodded, unashamed of the tears that ran freely down his cheeks. "I know, Abba, but they are all I have that I can give to the Saviour."

His father looked to the ground and then to the skies that had ripped open with the announcement of the birth of the King of Kings. "I will bring Esther, Son. You carry your perfect lamb."

Wondering While Wandering

The Roman Soldier

Mark 15:21-39

Mark 28:11-15

He shut the door and leaned against it. The streets were still raging, but the door did lessen the sounds. If only he could so easily shut the door on his raging thoughts, yet he doubted even time would ease them.

He dropped his armor in a pile, the breastplate on top. It could not protect his heart anymore. He crossed to his bed and sank. He tenderly fingered the folded cloth he held to his chest before he laid it at his side. Fumbling, he unlatched his shoes, let them thud to the floor, and slid them beneath the bed. The cold, rock floor felt good to his feet. He buried his head in his hands.

"Marcus, I heard your armor hit the floor..." Anna stopped. She gently placed her hand on his knee as she knelt before him. "Marcus, are you all right?"

He drew in a deep breath and dragged

his hands from his face before he whispered, "No."

Anna gasped, "You've a swollen, gashed, black eye and blood all over your hands. It was a bad day, wasn't it?"

"The worst. I am quitting as soon as this assignment is over, Anna."

"It is not over?"

"No, Anna. I don't know if it will ever be over. But I am to keep watch tonight over a dead man."

"A dead man?" Anna looked deeply into his eyes with question.

The soldier nodded. "A dead man. That outspoken group of religious lunatics claims someone will steal the body to say he rose from the dead." He shook his head. "On my watch? No. Not on my watch. No one will steal even a body on my watch, at least not without the help of God and a legion of angels." Marcus paused, "Really, I would be glad if God himself came to claim this man they call Jesus." Marcus felt a smile fumble at his lips as his thoughts raced. "You know, I hope God does come to get this man they call his Son!"

Wondering While Wandering

"Marcus, this is not like you. I've some water warm on the fire. Let's clean you, and we will talk about what did happen."

"Anna, these are things you should not hear. They are horrible."

His wife paused only a moment. "If you do not tell me about it, I will hear it on the streets. I can trust what you say to me, Marcus. There is no telling how it will sound from the streets."

Marcus sighed. "True. But I'll not take part in this wretched job again. Never again."

Anna wrung the cloth out and touched it to Marcus's eye. "Tell me about this black eye. It looks to need stitching."

He leaned back to give Anna a better angle to work. "Stitch away. You know, Anna, there must be a mighty strength in man when he knows he is about to die. He fought. He cursed. He bit. He spit, he slugged me, and I have the eye to remember him by. It took the three of us to get him tied. He deserved what he got. He was a murderer and a thief, but he fought every inch of the way."

Wondering While Wandering

"It's still hard, isn't it?" Anna dropped the bloody cloth back into the bowl of water. "I'll get the needle and thread."

Marcus nodded. "One has to be strong to follow some orders."

Marcus gripped the frame of the bed while Anna stitched. Neither spoke, and both were glad when the stitching was done.

Anna picked up Marcus's hands. "And this blood?" she asked.

Marcus let his eyes fall to his hands. He swallowed, and his voice shook when finally, he spoke. "Anna, this is not the blood of the thief and murderer. No, the blood is not his. This blood is from the one they called the King of the Jews. Anna, he was not tied to his cross. We were ordered to nail him to his death."

His wife gasped, "Nail him? You nailed him?"

Marcus nodded and ran his blood-dried hands through his hair. "Anna, never have I done a thing like this before, and, Anna, he did not fight me. He gave me his hand! He stretched his arm out and gave me his hand, and I took it. I took it and nailed it to that wooden beam." Marcus threw his hands over his face. He swallowed a sob before he could continue. "Anna, he watched me. He watched me in agony, but I think that agony was deeper than pounding a nail in his hand. There was more, much more. It was as if his eyes sank into...no... his eyes sliced far beyond my heart and into my soul, peeling back all the filthy layers of my sin! I think he knew everything I have ever done or even thought of doing. Anna," Marcus paused and licked his lips, "I feel he really was the son of God, and even worse, I killed him!" Marcus spread his hands and looked at them as if they were repulsive. "This is his blood, Anna. This is the Son of God's blood." Marcus shook his head, "I don't think it will wash off." Marcus swallowed then he stabbed his eyes into Anna's and whispered, "Before he took his last breath, Anna, I begged him to forgive me."

Anna held her hand over her mouth, but she could not utter a word.

Marcus shook his head, then continued, "His lips were swollen. We had given him vinegar with gall to drink, and...I don't think he could talk anymore. Not with his voice, but I swear he spoke with his eyes. His eyes forgave me. I think I still feel his eyes burning inside of me." Marcus again cradled his head in his bloody hands and shook.

"And, Anna, oh, the things that he said on that cross! Those things were not filled with hate. He struggled for breath just to utter, 'Father, forgive them; they know not what they do.' But his last words filled me with shame. 'It is finished' and 'Father, into thy hands I commend my spirit.' When those words were said, that was it. He died, but guilt was born and thrives in me."

Anna picked up the folded cloth beside her husband and wrapped it about him. She sat close beside him, "Marcus, do you really believe this was the Son of God?"

Slowly Marcus lifted his head and let his eyes settle on the blood of his hands. "Yes. My very being cries out that this truly was the Son of God...and I killed him."

Anna shook her head. "It was decreed, Marcus. It was not you. We, the people, killed him."

Wondering While Wandering

"But it was by my hand, Anna. I do not know how I shall live with that."

"No, Marcus." Anna reached for his hands to hold. "It was by our hands. We, the people, all of us, killed him. All of us killed the Son of God."

Marcus dropped his hands to his knees. He fingered the cloth about him, paled, and yanked it from his body, thrusting it in a wad at his feet. He struggled to speak, "This...this is his robe, Anna." He looked to the ceiling. "God forgive me, I won his robe by casting lots at the foot of his cross!"

Anna gasped as she stared at the bloody robe. Then she touched his cheek, "Marcus, I think you won more than just a cloak at the foot of that cross. I think you won your life and your soul on the battleground of that cross."

Lovingly, he reached down and pulled the garment to his chest, then twisted it about his shoulders. "You are right, Anna. As I am sheltered by his cloak, I know I am covered by his blood. Truly, this man was the Son of God."

Marcus slipped the robe from his

Wondering While Wandering

shoulders and draped it about his wife. "Keep his robe about you, Anna, while I guard his grave and wait for God himself to come to claim his Son. I am more than ready to witness miracles!"

After three long days and nights, Marcus burst through the door calling, "Anna! Anna!"

Anna dropped her basket and ran from the garden, "Marcus? Is all well?"

"Well? You tell me." Marcus yanked a bag from his pocket and dumped the contents on the table. Coins rolled and spattered, clinking over the wood.

Anna stared, "Silver? Marcus, where did you get this silver?"

He laughed. "From those religious lunatics."

"They paid you for watching the body? I thought those were your orders."

"Yes. Yes, it was my orders, but the body of the King of the Jews is gone."

Anna gasped. "Gone? No! Oh no! Marcus, can they take your life in place of a missing body? Your life for an escaped body?"

Again, Marcus laughed. "Anna, Jesus did not escape. He conquered death. Did you feel that earthquake early this morning?" Marcus boomed with excitement. "Jesus lives. I tell you; he lives! I saw it all! Truly, he is the Son of God. The religious leaders know it, but they will not admit it. They paid us, the guards, to say we fell asleep, and the Jews came and stole his body. And, Anna, they gave their word to protect us from the governor."

"Are you sure?" Anna whispered.

"Yes!"

Anna whispered, "But, Marcus, can you keep it secret?"

Marcus sobered. He looked deep into her eyes. "Anna, those religious leaders paid from their own treasury for the death of the Son of God. It is told all over the city that the one who sold Jesus to them hung himself. If I had not taken their silver, I am convinced I would already be a dead man. The only safe secret those religious leaders know is a secret sealed in the tomb. Anna, listen to me. That means I am but a dead man breathing borrowed air."

Wondering While Wandering

Anna paled and gasped, "Then, Marcus, we must go. I will go anywhere with you, but we must go now."

"Anna, you will not mind leaving your family, your home? You will come with me?"

"Yes, Marcus. You are a dead man if we stay. Of course, I will come with you. I will go anywhere as long as I am with you."

Marcus laughed. He grabbed his wife and swung her about the room until they collapsed on the cot. "I am sure of three things, Anna. First, we are rich, so rich that I can quit soldiering. Soldiering will not miss me, and I will not miss it. Second, Jesus Christ truly is the Son of God who has risen from the dead, and he forgives even men like me of their horrible deeds. And third, Anna, Anna, I love you so much and want you to know Jesus in the same way I know him."

Anna gently touched the robe she had washed and scrubbed while trying to remove the blood stains...the very blood of Jesus Christ. A shiver traveled through her body, and she was glad the stains were still etched forever in the garment. She nodded, "Yes, Marcus, I want this joy you have. You must show me how to meet Jesus."

King Solomon's Wisdom
I Kings 3:16-28

With a thud, the heavy cup was placed before her. Her breathing quickened. Would this solve her problem? Slowly, she reached for the chipped handle and pulled it closer. She looked into the depths and felt a shiver pass like something dark lurking over her shoulder. The murky liquid swirled slowly, birthing life of itself.

She closed her eyes and drifted back in time. It reminded her of pieces she had heard of King Solomon's writings. The writings were for his son, Jeroboam, who was to fill his father's shoes as king when King Solomon passed on. She had been huddled in the room's darkest corner, trying not to be seen by the crowd of half-drunken men. The man had raised his mug high and, with laughter, quoted King Solomon. "Who hath woe? who hath sorrow? who hath contentions? who hath babbling? who hath wounds without cause? who hath redness of eyes? They that tarry long at the wine; they that go to seek mixed wine. Look not thou upon the wine when it is red, when it giveth his colour in the cup, when it moveth itself aright. At the last it biteth like a serpent, and stingeth like an adder. Thine eyes shall behold strange women, and thine heart shall utter perverse things." Then he laughed and drained the cup dry.

Kedesha closed her eyes as she remembered. The man's gaze had roamed over the room, settled on her, and with dread, she had felt it like a smothering fog. He had swaggered over to stand above her. "I want strange, beautiful women, and I will start with you." He grabbed her up and held her tightly.

Kedesha shook her head to block out that horrible night, but she felt it would haunt her for the rest of her life. She hated herself almost as much as the women she worked with hated her for being his chosen one. They wished that man had chosen them. She wished it had been one of them, too, any of them, but no. He had chosen her.

She pulled her eyes from the depths of the cup. Her hand caressed her belly with the growing torment it held. Forever, she had wanted a babe. What Hebrew girl had not? A babe was a blessing from Jehovah. A blessing. This? Her hand trembled. A blessing? And she was sitting in this place to put an end to this blessing. A tear tripped over her eyelid and tip-toed down her cheek. Quickly, she swished it away.

From behind, the old woman shadowed over her and dragged the cup closer, yanking her again into the present. "Won't work if you don't drink it."

Kedesha put her elbows on the wooden table and rubbed her temples. Her stomach moved in circles, as did the thick liquid in the cup.

Across the table, Zered stared. "Kedesha, she is right. You do not want to have a baby, not without a husband. You do not even like this job. With a baby, the job will be worse."

Kedesha gazed into the cup, took a deep breath, and then looked up at the old, devious woman standing with her hands on her hips, waiting. Kedesha had to know. "Will it hurt?"

The woman's hair frizzled from beneath the head covering she wore as she tipped her head to the side. "Won't hurt you much. Might be sick a few days. Never heard how it feels to the babe, but it kills the babe just like that." The old woman snapped her fingers in the air. "No more worries."

Wondering While Wandering

Kedesha jumped. Her heart sped faster, and her face paled.

The old woman dipped her head closer and whispered, "I call it murder, murder of the innocent." She paused and winked, "But I get paid a plenty for it, and I ain't the one drinking the death brew."

Kedesha's eyes filled with pain. Her heart was running out the door, leaving her body in the cold room.

The woman dropped her brows and pronounced each word with her fingertip, tapping the wooden table. "Now, woman, you drink that cup, and your problems will be solved." She pushed the cup under Kedesha's nose.

The odor wafted in the air, making her stomach roll.

Zered asked the question Kedesha wanted to ask. "Does this always work?"

The old woman narrowed her eyes, "Murder the babe? That always work? It sure does. I have never had it fail."

"Good," Zered mumbled, picked up her cup, and sipped. Her face grimaced, and a shudder followed the swallow. She coughed. "That is a mighty strong brew. I felt the heat spread through my whole body."

Wondering While Wandering

The woman laughed. "Might be a bit strong. Your Master, Rueben, told me to be sure it worked. He said he didn't want your jobs to be interrupted beings how you two are some of the best he's got."

Zered looked up. "He did, did he?"

"Uh huh, he sure did," the woman nodded, looking from one to the other. "I gave him my word that this concoction would do the job."

Guilt washed over Kedesha, and she wished the old woman would go away. Her mind mulled over the word 'murder.' She closed her eyes. Always, she had wanted a babe, and now that she carried hope in her womb, she was here to kill it. Murder. She would be murdering her own child. Kedesha dropped her head in her hands and thought she would be sick.

Zered smiled. "You cannot drink it, can you?"

Kedesha groaned. "I dare not drink it, but I know what will happen if I don't, and I have no other place to go."

Zered took another sip of her cup. "You puzzle me. You are not made for this work. I think you hate the job."

"Hate it? I detest it."

Wondering While Wandering

Zered's lips stretched in a grim line. "How did you end up here?"

"My father. He followed Absalom, and he never came back. Rumors were that he died in the fight, but there was never any proof. It was the death of my mother. Our land went to my father's brother." She shrugged. "Family would not take me in. They feared their lands, and more would be taken because my father had followed Absalom."

Zered nodded. "I understand their fear. Those times were terrible."

"War is terrible. I had no place to go, and this place scooped me up. Master Reuben bought me to wait tables. He told my uncle that, and I waited on tables for a while. My uncle came to check on me a couple of times, but those times dwindled to never. I got older, and as our Master Reuben told me, 'The job is what it is. And if a good customer takes a shine to you, then that is what your job is.'" She closed her eyes and sighed. "The job saved my life, and yet it has taken my life from me. And the burden of guilt seems more than I can bear."

Zered narrowed her eyes, "You believe in Jehovah, don't you?"

Wondering While Wandering

Kedesha shivered, "With all my heart. I live in terror of judgment; judgment of this life I live and...and now...and now murder! Hell will be the only place that can warm my heart!" Her voice spiked on the word 'hell.'

From across the cold room, the old woman lifted her eyes. She sat down the pitcher she carried and headed in their direction. She leaned over the cold table, resting her hands on the rough wood, eyeing first one, then the other. "Everything all right?"

Zered came to the rescue, "Well, yes. I took a big gulp from this cup and likened the taste to the place we call hell. It is thick, hot, and mighty strong."

The old woman chuckled. "Like I said. It gets the job done." She studied both before she spoke, "Drink up," she hesitated and gave a sinister wink before she added with a chuckle, "Ladies."

Both women knew the slur on their character. Zered glared. Kedesha's cheeks flushed, and she dropped her head in shame.

The old woman laughed, turned, and walked away.

Wondering While Wandering

Across the table, her only friend watched the old lady at the other end of the room. When her back was toward them, she whispered, "Some say that old woman has a familiar spirit, and I think I believe that rumor."

Kedesha shivered.

Zered paused in thought before she continued. "Kedesha, I have a plan. If it works, you won't have to drink that cup."

Kedesha lifted her eyes, eager to listen.

"Kedesha, take a few sips from your cup, then pour the rest of the brew into the skirts of your garment. I will do the same."

"How is that going to help?" the terrified girl asked.

"I know our Master Reuben. He will check with the old woman. If we both are still with child, he will think the old woman's brew did not do the job he paid it to do. But it will be too late to drink the brew when he finds out it did not work."

"What happens to us?"

Wondering While Wandering

Zered sighed. "We will get the duty of cooking, marketing, drawing water, cleaning, washing, and the list goes on."

Kedesha closed her eyes and nodded. "We will be doing all the chores."

Zered tipped her head and shrugged.

"I would rather do the chores anytime. But," she paused and looked directly into Zered's eyes, "we get to have the babies?"

Zered nodded. "Yes. We have the babies."

"Master Reuben will allow the babies?"

Zered took a long pull of air. "Kedesha. There will be a price to pay. For me, I have a plan for my child. I know the father of my baby. I know his wife would give anything to have a baby. I think I can get the father to pay me a good bit of silver for this baby I carry, especially if it is a boy."

Kedesha narrowed her eyes. "Master Reuben will allow that?"

"I know he will. He loves the sound of silver and gold coins clinking. Oh, he will take a good share of my earnings, but I will still come out ahead."

Wondering While Wandering

Kedesha bit her bottom lip, thinking about Zered's plan. Finally, she asked, "And my babe?"

Zered leaned back and smiled. "Kedesha, everyone knows who your baby's father is, except Master Reuben. The father is royalty. Some say he could even be Jeroboam, the King's son himself. If Master Reuben had known, he would never have sent you to the old woman. You carry valuable merchandise. Surely, the father of your baby would pay a hefty amount of silver to hush up your baby's identity."

Kedesha's heart pounded. "Then he must not find out. Promise me, Zered."

She shrugged. "I can only give my word for myself. And we can only hope the others don't talk."

"That will take a miracle," Kedesha breathed.

Zered smirked, "Pray to your Jehovah God. I hear he is a miracle worker."

Kedesha trembled. Would Jehovah God even listen to her, being the kind of woman she was? Her hope had no solid foundation, but she had nowhere else to turn. Her heart pleaded, "Jehovah God, please keep my babe's identity safe from this torturous world, and please forgive me."

Zered looked at Kedesha in wonder, then she pushed the cup, reminding her to take a sip so her breath would reek of the murdering brew.

Kedesha sipped and felt her cheeks burn, spreading warmth throughout her body. The flutter in her womb caught her breath. It was the first time her babe had made known his presence. She then vowed before Jehovah God that she would protect this child with her life if need be. Gently, she eased the cup to the side of her chair and oozed the liquid into the skirts of her garments. Then, one last time, she brought the cup to her lips as the ole woman passed. She sat the cup down with a thud and heaved. She threw one hand over her mouth and one hand across her stomach.

The old woman stopped and chuckled, "Told you it was mighty powerful. You'll be rid of that baby in no time. If my brew should come up," she warned, "I gave my word to your master, I would make you another." She swept up the cup and left.

Kadesh whispered. "I believe she does carry a familiar spirit, or maybe a familiar spirit carries her."

Wondering While Wandering

Life, horrible life, went on as usual until Master Reuben discovered the wicked brew had not done its deed. "That old woman will pay for this," he vowed pounding the counter.

Zered slipped a tiny smile in Kedesha's direction, and their life changed.

For the next months, she worked from daylight until deep in the night and even through the night if someone called. Her hands were red and raw. Bags bulged beneath her eyes. Her feet were swollen and ached. Her only comfort was when she felt the miracle of her babe moving. When no one was around, she sang the songs of her childhood to the babe she carried.

Master Reuben hovered like a vulture. He cursed the old woman, but Kedesha watched his eyes glint when they landed on Zered. She knew the deal with the father of Zered's baby had been made, and the Master was counting the coins, the weight of silver he would get from Zered's baby.

Master Reuben had asked her if she knew the father of the child she carried. She had lied, hid the surprise that he had not discovered who the father was, and thanked Jehovah God that he had not.

Wondering While Wandering

She was on her knees scrubbing the stones of the floor when she felt Master Reuben's shadow fall over her. "Kedesha, I want to know who you think the father might be."

She tossed the rag into the bowl, put her hands on her knees, and stretched her back. That always felt so good. She closed her eyes and slowly shook her head. "Master, I do not know."

He glared. "You were told to keep track of names, times, and dates because sometimes it will benefit the both of us."

"Yes, Master. You had just changed my duties, and all this was new. I did not keep a list."

"You will from now on." He spat on her clean floor. Then he turned and tromped away muttering, "I'll find a buyer."

Kedesha drew in a quick breath. A buyer? For her babe? Her chest felt like it was going to cave in. She had nothing in this world and began to think this child was all she might ever have. This baby was hers. She would not give her baby up. She would have to go somewhere, anywhere, but she wanted her baby.

Wondering While Wandering

That was when the first pain ripped through her body. She went ridged and held her breath. She counted all the way to seven before it eased. Wringing out the rag, she wiped the Master's spital from the cold floor, stood, and picked up the bowl of water to toss out the door.

Kedesha needed to find Zered. They had agreed they would help each other when the time came. But would Zered go further and help her escape?

She swirled the dirty water in the bowl and threw it to the side of the door. A stronger pain racked her body. She doubled over and began the count. Twelve. No fifteen. No. The contraction would not ease, and at twenty-seven, she sank to the ground and quit counting. When she pulled herself upright and staggered around the corner of the tavern and to the small house, she shared with Zered she did not know. She closed the door behind her, stumbled to the bedroom, and dropped. Another contraction wracked her body. She did not even try to count this time; rather, she shoved her pillow in her mouth and clamped it tight. She heaved in great gulps of air and prayed to Jehovah above. This was work like she had never done before. She quivered. This was work that would produce life, the life of her own child. Time raced, and time stood still. The sun passed over the thatched roof, and evening shadows fell. The pain was eased only long enough to catch her breath and start another contraction. She dared not cry out if she planned to leave this place.

Alone, she had her babe. Alone, she wiped and wrapped him in soft, baby garments she had prepared. She held him close and felt the warmth of someone she loved...someone she would live and die for. She held him to her breast and whispered, "No, no, do not cry my little one."

Kedesha was alone, and it felt as though she had always been alone. Maybe it was better this way. Maybe she could take this wonderful, beautiful baby boy and leave this life behind. Maybe.

But the next day, they found her and her baby boy. Zered was pulled away from the life of chores they led to take care of Kedesha and her babe, and someone was given to watch the door. Master Reuben said it was for any needs they might have. Kedesha knew it was to hinder any thoughts of escape.

Three days later, Zered gave birth to a healthy baby boy.

Wondering While Wandering

The Master gave them a few days of peace; then they had to take care of their cleaning, scrubbing, and cooking. They took turns. One would stay with the babies. The other would work. Every few hours, they would switch.

Kedesha opened the door and tip-toed in. Zered held her son and stared into his sleeping face. "He is beautiful." She whispered.

Kedesha smiled as she knelt beside her own son. "Zered, how are you going to sell your son?"

Zered licked her lips. "Kedesha, he is beautiful, but that does not mean I want to keep him. It means he will be worth more silver." Then she tipped her head to the side. "Kedesha, your baby is beautiful, too. You will get more silver for him."

Kedesha's heart pounded. Soon, she had to escape from here with her baby boy, but she dared not say a word to Zered. Any trust she had had of Zered as a friend was gone.

That night, she went to the tiny window. Maybe she could squeeze through it. Maybe. She would wait until Zered slept solidly. She would nurse her baby, wrap him tightly, and gently ease him from the window to the ground. Then, she would carefully squeeze through the opened window herself.

Kedesha laid beside her babe and snuggled close. She could feel his sweet breath on her neck. What a miracle Jehovah had allowed. She took a long, deep pull of air and whispered 'thank yous' over and over to the Jehovah God of her people.

She closed her eyes and listened for the simple snoring Zered made from her room when her sleep was deep. But it was she who slept.

A ray of sunshine slipped over her face, teasing her with its morning light. A gentle breeze danced with the filmy curtains. Kedesha stretched. She turned to her baby boy, smiled, and touched his soft cheek.

Kedesha froze. His cheek was cold. She threw the covers aside and scooped her babe into her arms. He was cold all over. She rushed to the window and held her babe to the dusky dawn. Her babe was blue in the pale light. "NO! NO! Jehovah, No!" She held him high and shook him hoping for some life to jump inside him.

Nothing happened. She gasped and pulled her cold babe close. But what could she expect? She knew what she was, and she knew who Jehovah was. Why would He bless her? She wailed as a barrage of tears cascaded down her cheeks. Jehovah had taken her babe.

Zered was by her side. "Kedesha, settle down. What is wrong?"

Tears ran in torrents. Her voice was jilted. "My babe! My babe! My baby boy is dead!"

Zered stood back, and as a matter of fact, she quietly spoke, "You must have laid on him while you slept."

"What?" Kedesha shook.

"Your baby. You must have laid on your baby while you slept. You must have smothered him." Zered explained.

Slowly, Kedesha pulled her baby from her chest. The now bright light from the window shone on his face. She gulped, shoved her baby into Zered's arms, and backed away from her friend. "No! No!" She turned and bolted from her room and into Zered's bedroom. She grabbed the baby from the bed and rushed to the window for the full light. This baby was her child. Not Zered's, and Zered knew it.

Wondering While Wandering

Zered swept through the doorway. "Give me my baby, Kedesha."

"He is not your baby, Zered. He is mine, and you know it! You are the one that laid on your baby in your sleep, not me."

"Prove it," Zered's eyes were hard and cold. "It will be my word against yours, Kedesha, and Master Reuben will believe me because he will profit more if that baby is mine."

"You do not love your baby. I love mine," Kedesha shoved past Zered and ran from the house.

"Give me my baby!" Zered yelled and followed. She grabbed the mother's arm and swung her around. "Kedesha! That baby is my future! He is all I have! Do not ruin it for me!"

"This babe is my son; he is all I have!" Kedesha shook.

A crowd gathered and surrounded the two women. Master Reuben shoved through. "Stop it. Both of you. Stop it now!" He grabbed each woman by the arm and separated them. "What goes on?"

Zered planted her hands on her hips and spat accusing words. "She took my baby and will not give him back. She laid on hers while they slept and smothered him, so she grabbed up my baby and took him."

"That is not true," Kedesha shouted. "She overlaid her baby."

Master Reuben narrowed his eyes, looking from one woman to the other. He grinned as he made his decision. "Kedesha, give the baby to Zered."

Zered stood tall and held her arms wide, waiting for the baby. A smirk twitched at her lips. She whispered, "I told you Master Reuben would stand with me."

"I will not give my baby to her." Kedesha simmered, ready to overflow. "He is my child!"

The babe started crying.

The surrounding crowd began choosing sides and shouting.

From outside the gathering, a voice thundered, "What goes on here?"

Kedesha's heart froze. Quickly, she dipped her head and bowed.

The horde of people around her did the same.

Wondering While Wandering

The man arrayed in royal garments on a black steed cut through the throng. "I asked what is going on?"

Master Reuben spoke. "It is a misunderstanding between my, a, my ladies here. Both have babies, and one mother laid on her baby in the night. But both claim the live child and say the dead child belongs to the other. I know the two women, and I believe the child belongs to this woman." He pulled Zered to stand beside him.

Kedesha exploded. "This is not her babe. He is mine, and he is all I have! I will not give him to her."

"She knows he is my baby," Zered's eyebrows rose like royalty over her eyes.

The crowd started milling and churning into life.

"Enough!" the man on the horseback ordered. He looked from one woman to the other. He studied Kedesha a bit longer, trying to place her, then furrowed his brows when the babe began squalling. The man, he had heard him called Reuben, carried a shady look, one of distrust. Yet he did not really care who the baby belonged to, but it might be interesting to see how their wise King would handle judgment on this squabble. After all, King

Wondering While Wandering

Solomon was heralded the wisest man the world had ever known. "The King stands in the judgment hall now. Bring the child and follow me." He turned his horse, and all followed.

The horseman cut to the front of the line in the judgment hall to address the King. "King Solomon," he dismounted and bowed low, "these two harlots both claim this child. Maybe you can discern who the child rightfully belongs to." The challenge was laid.

Master Reuben brought the women forward to stand before the King.

Kedesha knelt.

Zared quickly followed suit.

King Solomon nodded. "What is the problem?"

Kedesha trembled, but she stood fast, holding her babe close. "O my lord, I and this woman dwell in one house; and I was delivered of a child with her in the house. And it came to pass the third day after that I was delivered, that this woman was delivered also: and we were together; there was no stranger with us in the house, save we two in the house. And this woman's child died in the night; because she overlaid it. And she arose at midnight, and took my son from beside me, while thine handmaid slept, and laid it in her bosom, and laid her dead child in my bosom. And when I rose in the morning to give my child suck, behold, it was dead: but when I had considered it in the morning, behold, it was not my son, which I did bear."

Zered pushed beside Kedesha and broke in, "Nay; but the living is my son, and the dead is thy son."

Kedesha shook her head. "No; but the dead is thy son, and the living is my son."

King Solomon held his hand for silence before he spoke. "The one saith, This is my son that liveth, and thy son is the dead: and the other saith, Nay; but thy son is the dead, and my son is the living." He paused and studied the two women before him. He looked above to the Lord God Jehovah, smiled, and the king ordered, "Bring me a sword."

A soldier brought a sword before the king.

In a bold voice, King Solomon commanded, "Divide the living child in two, and give half to the one, and half to the other."

Wondering While Wandering

A gasp spread over the crowded court.

The soldier yanked Kedesha's babe from her arms and dangled him by an ankle from the air.

The jolted babe bawled.

"No!" Kedesha's heart ripped apart.

The soldier whipped his sword from the sheath and swung it high.

Gasps filled the judgment hall.

Kedesha's bowels yearned upon her son, and she cried, "O my lord, give her the living child, and in no wise slay it!"

Zered gloated, "Let it be neither mine nor thine, but divide it."

Then the king pointed his golden scepter to Kedesha and said, "Give her the living child, and in no wise slay it: she is the mother thereof."

Silence filled the judgment hall like a quilt on a cold night, and just as suddenly, great awe of the wisdom of King Solomon moved through the people, for they saw that the wisdom of God was in him to do judgment.

Wondering While Wandering

Kedesha took her babe from the soldier's hand and held him tightly to her bosom. "Shhh," she hushed her bellowing son as she knelt down before royalty and thanked King Solomon. Then she lifted her eyes to Jehovah and praised his name.

A hand reached out from her side to help her from the cold tiles. She stood and turned to the man.

The man of royalty tightened his eyes and looked deeply into hers. "Do I know you?"

Wondering While Wandering

Thank you for reading my book. I hope you enjoyed the characters and found yourself involved in the story.

I would appreciate if you would write a review on Amazon and other online bookstores for each of my books you have read.

Would love to hear from you at:

Slaurel11478@gmail.com

www.gwcowboypreacher.com

Sandra Waggoner